ALSO BY ASH LINGAM

WINTER SOLSTICE

WINTER SOLSTICE

A YA WESTERN NOVELLA

ASH LINGAM
GERALD L. GUY

WISE WOLF
BOOKS

WISE WOLF BOOKS
An Imprint of Wolfpack Publishing
wisewolfbooks.com
1707 E. Diana Street
Tampa, FL 33610

Paperback ISBN 978-1-965596-12-8
eBook ISBN 978-1-965596-11-1

PREFACE

Here's a news flash. When authors are not spending long hours creating plots and interesting characters, they are reading the works of other novelists.

Authors are no different from anyone else. We become rabid fans of our favorite authors and the characters they create.

That's how "Tonkawa Christmas" came about.

I became a Texas Ranger fan when I picked up my first Ash Lingam novel. I fell in love with Captain Rowdy Bates, "One-Eyed" Jack Black, and likable Bill Vents.

I contacted Lingam when his Tonkawa series began because its originality was captivating, and I wanted him to know I was a fan. To my surprise, Lingam had read my McIntyre Adventure series. A friendship developed and, before long, we began discussing a joint project. If you are reading this, you are aware of the results. The joint effort fell together in a matter of weeks.

To make it work, I developed the characters of

Tommy Turnbolt and Delbert Fisher Elliot, two young misfits from a traveling freak show who are rescued by Lingam's "odd couple," Potak and Tuc.

Could there be an odder foursome?

Tommy and Del are White teenagers, one tall and one small. The Tonkawa cousins are seasoned veterans of the Indian Wars. Potak is a medicine man, and Tuc is a fierce warrior.

The orphaned teens are naïve newcomers to the wild country of the American southwest. Their journey begins when a fortune teller informs them they can find their long-lost parents in Texas. Potak and Tuc are guided by visions Potak conjures up at will as the two, crusty old-timers search for their own destinies. Magic happens when their paths cross on a frigid Texas night.

Ash and I hope you enjoy this latest edition of the Tonkawa saga as much as we enjoyed creating it. And Merry Christmas!

"It is not in the stars to hold our destiny but in ourselves."
—**William Shakespeare**

WINTER SOLSTICE

1. WINTER'S ARRIVAL

Seminole Canyon, Texas Panhandle

IN ONE AFTERNOON, THE TEMPERATURES DROPPED OVER thirty degrees. Surprisingly enough, sometimes it got extremely cold in West Texas. It wasn't every year, but upon occasion, the temperatures plunged to unbearable depths. The panhandle region, farthest from the Gulf of Mexico, experiences colder winters than the other regions of the state. Occasional Arctic blasts can cause thermometers to plunge well below freezing and bring snowy conditions.

Tonkawa warrior Tuc welcomed the relief from the normal Texas heat. His medicine man cousin, Potak, deplored the change in temperature. The warrior had his bearskin tied to his waist and only wore his buckskin shirt and leggings. Potak had donned every piece of clothing he owned. He had his bearskin wrapped around his shoulders and high over his neck to cover his ears.

They came to West Texas late in the year because it

was a place where they could see important visions that, perhaps, would show them the path they would follow in the spring, when all was renewed.

"This must be close to the time our Texas Rangers friends call Christmas," Potak said with a red nose. "In the Indian Nations, we observe the winter solstice, which has been a period of reverence since ancient times. For Indigenous peoples all over the West, it is a time to offer gratitude, honor family and ancestors, and to follow our sacred rituals and beliefs."

Potak yawned as he had heard his cousin repeat the same thing year after year, as though he might forget such an important event. He grumbled but held his tongue and forged onward as he enjoyed the bitter cold air against his face. A warrior could endure all types of weather. He never let such things affect his awareness and skills. Tuc prided himself on being at his best in every situation, from snow blizzards to sweltering droughts and even sandstorms. He could navigate his way in each and was still just as deadly. His skills never faltered regardless of the climatic situation. He once battled an enemy in the middle of a hailstorm.

Potak was affected more and more by the winter weather with each passing year. He suffered from what White men called arthritis or stiff joints. The Indians called this ailment age. As they made their way down the Seminole Canyon, the old medicine man munched on herbs he had grown, which reduced the pain. He could only hope it would not snow before they got to shelter. Then, the cold in his feet could become unbearable.

Theological historians also place significance in the winter solstice, during which Christians celebrate

Christmas. A few days before the solstice, many American Indian tribes make prayer sticks in honor of ancestors or a native deity. They plant these sticks during a ceremony that welcomes the winter solstice. Usually, these native festivities occur in the White man's calendar on December 21 or 22, depending on the astrological configuration and the year. Many tribes host dances, bonfires at sunset, and festivals that celebrate family units, large and small.

Tuc and Potak were on yet another spiritual quest as they climbed higher up the valley of Seminole Canyon. Potak chose the route after a vision promised hope. Tuc argued against it, but the medicine man got his way. So they were seeking out the Tonkawa spirits in the wilderness. Potak's vision indicated they should seek cooler temperatures. The medicine man knew immediately where to go. When they got to the sacred place, the vision promised the shaman he would have yet another that would clarify the cousins' future.

Both men now bore bear skins to protect them from the cold as the temperatures continued to drop even lower. They had rarely experienced such weather during the sixty years they had roamed the earth. Potak claimed this extreme cold happened every seven years. Seven is an auspicious number for the Tonkawa tribe and other native people across the West. The dropping temperature often coincided with the day the White men celebrate the coming of their God, the one they call Christ.

They were in Seminole, Texas, over two hundred and fifty miles northeast of El Paso. The mountainous terrain regularly registered Texas's lowest annual temperature, sometimes dipping to minus twenty-two degrees. Minus thirty degrees was reached on occasion. Shivering, Potak believed it felt even colder.

Neither Tuc nor Potak possessed a thermometer, nor did they have an understanding of White man's temperatures. Even a fool knows when water freezes and the environment is dangerous for most living things. When the chill reached Potak's old bones, he sensed colder days were to come, and he knew well that the West Texas cold could be life-threatening if they were not prepared when it arrived in full force.

"I believe we better find a cave to hide in so we can build a fire out of the wind. We need to warm our bones," Potak said as he looked at the gray sky and pulled his bearskin tighter. "We can use the old shaft we sheltered in the last time we climbed these walls. I believe a blizzard will hit soon."

"We will have to go farther down the canyon," Tuc replied as he tried to peer into the distance, although it was impossible to see very far in the haze caused by the extreme weather. "I remember the place you mean. It is a short distance from here."

"We will have to move quickly," Potak said as he picked up more firewood and slipped it into Tuc's backpack. Tuc, in turn, put two more pieces in Potak's. They were both nearly full.

Tuc moved quickly through the afternoon. Potak swore under his breath every time he stubbed his toe on an ice-cold rock. In such temperatures, his bones ached and creaked with each step. Generally, in the heat of the plains, he didn't notice his age so much. His joints didn't groan with each step, and he didn't feel his weight against his hips, knees, and ankles. Now, he longed for his beloved warm weather. In such cold temperatures, his arthritis flared, and he easily chilled to the bone.

As they made their way toward their refuge and possible escape from the snowstorm, dark, heavy clouds indicated it would arrive shortly. They collected more firewood until their loads were just bearable. Five years ago, during their last visit, they left ample kindling and wood in the cave for their next visit. Few people lived in or traveled through the region. Their cave was all but impossible to locate unless one accidentally stumbled onto its location, or it was shown to them.

Finally, they arrived just below the rock face that led to their refuge. They clawed their way upward on a broken path that had deteriorated over the years but was still passable. Once they arrived halfway up the face of the canyon, the opening became visible. There was a flat landing in front of the cave with signs of an ancient campfire from long ago and warmer times. As soon as they entered the dark, dank-smelling cave, Potak lit the torch he had prepared for this occasion. Then, he went about making an enormous fire to warm his joints. His teeth chattered. The fire sat between them and the cave's entrance. As he fumbled with his fire-starting kit, Tuc pushed him aside with a kind smile and nimbly sparked the ball of kindling to life and placed it under the teepee of wood. He blew on the glowing embers until they grew and burst into flame. In minutes, the fire lashed out at the cold surrounding it. What was dark and dank moments earlier became a brightly lit shelter.

By the time he was done, the entrance to the old cave glowed like a beacon into the night. The Tonkawa weren't worried an enemy would show up in such an out-of-the-way place and on such a dreadful day. Any intelligent Indian would be keeping warm in his teepee with his woman.

"You would have to pick the worst day of the year to decide to come here," Tuc grumbled. "You know how you suffer the cold. We should have made our sacred journey into Mexico, where the mountains are warmer."

"I don't choose the time or place of visions," Potak retorted. "The Indian spirits choose the times, and, for them, it is the same if it is hot or cold. The Tonkawa spirits don't feel the weather like humans. They often pick these times to play with us so they can observe our folly. We could have ignored their message, but it is not wise to let visions go untended. What if it is a warning of imminent danger in our future?"

As the fire began to roar, images moved in the deep crevasse in the cave's ceiling, and the bats started to stir and flap their wings in protest of the intrusion. They were reluctant to move from the safe place where they hid. As the light violated their domain, a few startled and flew for the exit but returned shortly to the shelter of the cave. Blasts of Arctic wind blew past the entrance. The Indians and the bats waited out the storm together. Both species were at the mercy of Mother Nature, and both welcomed the warmth provided by the enormous fire. Potak put some more wood on the pile as gusts of freezing wind swirled outside. With each passing hour, the velocity of the wind increased. Before nightfall, they saw the first snowflakes. They were like millions of small feathers floating down from the heavens and quickly accumulating on the ground. In an hour, the landing at the front of the cave was covered in an inch of snow.

"If you make that fire any bigger, you're gonna burn us out," Tuc grumbled.

He removed his buckskin shirt due to the heat the blaze produced. Sweat shone on his aged skin. Hard muscle rippled below the surface. Potak sat as close as possible to the fire so the heat rolled over his face and body. He welcomed the fiery feeling. His joints began to loosen, and his teeth stopped chattering.

The medicine man pulled a coffee kettle from his backpack, filled it with water, and placed it on a rock right next to the coals. In minutes, the aroma of the dark brew mixed with that of burning wood in the enclosure. Soon, each Indian had a hot tin cup of boiling coffee in their hands. The heat transmitted to the shaman's old fingers and gave him even more relief from his arthritis.

"I don't like the cold anymore," Potak said. "It appears that we are aging differently, cousin."

"Use your ally—smoke—to take you to a warmer place," Tuc suggested. He knew the power of the herbal mix his cousin carried in this tobacco tin. "Maybe it will reveal the rest of your vision now that we are here, as the spirits requested."

2. MISFITS AND MARVELS

Somewhere in Western Texas

TOMMY TURNBOLT AND DELBERT ELLIOTT WERE THE original odd couple. One large and one small, they were two of the many misfits and oddballs who accompanied two dozen wagons across the Santa Fe Trail in the summer of 1878. The trek strained every resource available to the Marvelous Marvels Touring Company of Hannibal, Missouri.

Owner Ichabod Justice was in the process of relocating his touring company to California, the land of opportunity. He had grown weary of traipsing north and south annually to find suitable weather. The northern states were too cold in the winter and the southern states too hot in the summer. In California, the weather was reportedly fabulous all year long. Ichabod decided it would be the perfect place to set up business with his troupe of misfits, outrageous performers, and oddities.

The entrepreneur had stopped his caravan for repairs at a junction along the Arkansas River, a spot where most wagon trains either turned west to go to California or south to New Mexico. Tommy and Delbert, orphans who were as different as day and night, did everything they could to ensure every wagon made the grueling trip across the untamed Kansas Territory. There were two dozen wagons in the Justice caravan when they left Independence, Missouri. They lost only two along the rutted path that led west. The trek strained and tested the stamina of the performers and their livestock.

If not for the efforts of the two versatile teenagers, several wagons would not have made it past the halfway point, especially the wagon of lovable Miss Hutchins. She had been a surrogate mother to the two boys who were born into the Marvelous Marvels family years earlier. Both their mothers had been performers.

Delbert was just a baby when he was abandoned, and his care was transferred to Miss Hutchins. Tommy came along a half dozen or so years later when he was nine years old.

Delbert, like his mother, was extremely short. He was ten years old before he was able to grab a piece of toast from a tabletop. Tommy was the opposite. He was an inch short of six feet and a month short of his tenth birthday when his mother disappeared. Delbert begged Miss Hutchins to take custody of the gangly youngster and his best friend. She did with the approval of Justice, who became a father figure to both boys.

Hutchins, like almost everyone in the caravan, was an odd but loving woman. To say she was obese was an understatement. Ichabod promoted her as the "World's Largest Woman: One Thousand Pounds of Feminine Fancy." It was an exaggeration, as was most of the proclamations Justice made about his cast of Marvels, but she weighed every bit of six hundred pounds by the time the caravan began its trek west.

When the boys were just twelve years old, it was their job to transport her to the stage whenever the caravan pulled into a town for a performance. Miss Hutchins could no longer get along on her own because her legs could not support her massive weight. So, their roles changed. Tommy and Delbert became the caregivers, gladly reciprocating the kindness of Miss Hutchins, who had shown them so much love when they were younger.

They were the perfect pair for the job because Tommy was big and strong, and Delbert was intelligent and good with his hands. It was he who devised the winch system that respectfully lifted Miss Hutchins to the stage whenever she had to perform. Tommy provided the muscle.

Now sixteen years old and skilled at a variety of tasks, Justice depended on the teens and a pair of aging roustabouts to keep the train moving westward on the rugged Santa Fe Trail. They used their ingenuity and brute strength to solve most problems that popped up.

That's how things were among the carnival family. They cared for each other. Most of the actors were strange characters or odd-looking. That's what attracted the masses to Ichabod's shows. They had been shunned or mistreated by the general public before they joined the cast of Marvelous Marvels. Among people of their own kind, they found love and acceptance. They were no longer odd because everybody in the troupe was odd. They were loved and appreciated for their uniqueness.

* * *

BY THE TIME Tommy and Delbert were teenagers, they fit in perfectly with the troupe. Of course, it was the only life they knew. They recognized they made an odd pair, one just shy of four feet tall and the other pushing seven feet. The boys had grown up together—in fact, they were inseparable—and never gave much thought to their difference in height because all of the Marvelous Marvels were different in one way or another.

Ichabod used his collection of marvels to attract customers to his shows as they traveled from town to town. They provided a peek at the stranger side of Mother Nature. When Tommy and Del finished setting up the carnival tents and stages, it was their job to drum up business for opening night. Tommy would carry Delbert on his shoulder and walk through the streets of the towns they visited. The diminutive Delbert would become a "barker."

"Come one! Come all!" he called out in a high-pitched voice for all to hear. "Ichabod Justice invites you to be entertained by the Marvelous Marvels Touring Company this weekend."

People pointed and whispered to each other at the sight of the unlikely pair, but the promotion worked. When the carnival opened for business, there were always long lines of curious onlookers willing to pay a few pennies, a nickel, or a dime to see something they could see nowhere else.

Along with the world's largest woman, Justice's Marvels included a strong man, a fortune teller, a Persian queen, dinosaur bones, an albino Indian chief, a two-headed goat, and countless other oddities and performers.

Tommy and Del became integral pieces of the crew that set up and tore down whenever Justice stopped to perform. They also took admission, cared for livestock, and helped wherever needed.

They were not performers, even though it was obvious they were misfits, one too tall and the other too short.

They were born down around Missouri way, in a dirty little hole called Hannibal. Delbert's mama died giving birth, as occurred all too often in the nineteenth century. Birthing children was not easy. Doctors were few, and prenatal care was not what it is today. Twenty-five percent of the women who gave birth to children in the 1800s didn't survive the delivery. Estar Elliott, rest her soul, was one of them.

Delbert's mother was only three feet six inches tall and was recognized as the "World's Shortest Woman." His father, Jack Elliott, was taller than six feet and one of the show's laborers. He raised the tents, cared for the animals, fixed anything that needed repair, and took admission at many of the shows.

Miss Hutchins said Estar was the kindest woman she ever met. Estar and Delbert's father instantly fell in love. Their height and weight differential never seemed to matter to the loving couple. They lived a normal life, despite being the only married couple in Ichabod's touring company. Miss Hutchins said seeing them together spread joy and hope through the rest of the entourage.

"I always thought if Estar and Jack could fall in love, I too might find a partner one day," Miss Hutchins explained. She didn't, of course, but she did get to care for a child when Ichabod placed Estar's child in her arms. She considered it a blessing and became the only mother the toddler ever knew.

When Jack Elliott lost his wife to childbirth, he was more than heartbroken. He was distraught. It was shortly after that he ran afoul of the law and was incarcerated, a secret Miss Hutchins kept from the child. She told Delbert his father ran off because his son was such a tiny baby. He presumed the child would be a dwarf like his mother, and the sight of him reminded him too much of his beloved wife. He deserted Delbert and the others without saying a word.

Tommy's upbringing was quite different from Delbert's. He had no idea who his father was, but his mother was one of Ichabod's top attractions, breathtakingly beautiful, and Justice's one and only "Bearded Lady."

Most women consider childbirth a blessing. Not Tommy's mother. The vain and curvaceous Emily Turnbolt made Tommy call her "M" because she didn't want to be addressed by anything that indicated she was a mother.

"I never saw a mother who wasn't overweight and sagging in all the wrong places," M used to say. "I'm not, and I refuse to be lumped in a class of lesser women."

Tommy's mother thought she was better than everyone because she made lots of money for old Ichabod. She was an inch short of six feet tall, had sandy hair, blue eyes, and the most shapely figure of anyone on the carnival circuit. She kept her beard neatly trimmed and, during her shows, let one lucky visitor pull on it to prove it was real. When she bent to offer up her whiskers, she flashed cleavage that made most men drool.

Her beauty is what coerced so many men to spend a dime for a peek at her behind the Marvel's curtain as often as five times a day. It never failed. When the carnival rolled into a new town that was short on available young women, strangers fell instantly in love with M, beard and all.

Tommy became an orphan at nine years old. Two drunken cowboys snuck into their tent late one night outside of Kansas City and kidnapped M. Tommy was there when it happened. He was tied and gagged so he couldn't make a ruckus and forced to watch as they manhandled his mother. He said the first thing they did was strip her naked and shave off her golden beard. She fought like an alley cat, Tommy said, because that beard was what put food on their table.

Years later, Tommy remarked about how beautiful his mother was without the beard. Of course, he thought she was gorgeous with a beard too. She was statuesque but not tall like Tommy. He figured he inherited his size from the father he never knew.

Delbert was shocked when he walked into the Turnbolt tent to find his friend bound and gagged and his mother missing. Tommy never knew what happened to her. Was she taken far away or killed? Miss Hutchins said she suspected M was sold into bondage in a foreign land. She said something called "the sex trade" was big in the West.

Ichabod was heartbroken when M was stolen. He reported her disappearance to the local authorities, who sent out search parties, but she was never recovered. Some of the performers suspected it was Ichabod who impregnated M, but he never showed any special attention to Tommy before or after his mother's disappearance.

Delbert was glad Ichabod did not leave Tommy behind when the caravan left Kansas City because the two boys had become best friends, even though they were as different as night and day.

3. MYSTICAL ENCOUNTER

Traveling with the Carnival

THE CARNIVAL WAS ALL THE TWO BOYS KNEW. WHILE disagreements and jealousies existed, all the actors and crew happily performed their duties. Dancing and celebrating took place after every profitable engagement. When Ichabod's troupe was at the height of its popularity, he had thirty wagons in his traveling caravan.

He found new acts everywhere. When the weather got cold, Ichabod always directed the Marvelous Marvels south to avoid frigid temperatures. Normally, he wintered in Louisiana or Mississippi.

Throughout his travels, Ichabod was always looking for oddities: magicians, escape artists, sword swallowers, ancient fossils, or mammoth bones he could claim belonged to dinosaurs.

In Louisiana, he found a fortune teller and a Persian goddess, who claimed to once be part of a rich sheik's harem in the Middle East.

In Oklahoma, a wild-eyed farmer brought a two-headed goat that made both men and women gasp when they paid two pennies to see it. It was a freak of nature, created by tainted water on the outskirts of the Indian Territories, the farmer said. It was rumored Justice paid him twenty-five dollars for the goat, but nobody knew for sure. That was a lot of money.

In Arkansas, Justice discovered a beggar and outcast who became "White Devil: The Apache War Chief." His real name was Harold Cunningham. He was the oddest man Tommy and Delbert had ever seen.

Harold was shunned because he was an albino, a human whose skin pigment lacked all color. He was as pale as the powder Miss Hutchins used on her cheeks and had long, silvery hair and pink eyes that gave young children nightmares.

Ichabod dressed him up like an Indian. He was bare-chested and fitted with a loincloth that covered his privates, front and back. He wore a couple of eagle feathers in his hair and war paint on his face to make him look like a real Indian from out west. Everybody knew about Indians because the newspapers and dime novels were filled with tales of the harrowing attacks against White settlers.

People who paid a nickel for a peek at White Devil got a warning from Ichabod before they walked behind the curtain, where he sat with his back to the crowd and wrapped in a black blanket. He usually had a small campfire simmering. Justice, who was quite a showman, always introduced him with the same warning: "Chief White Devil has killed hundreds of men, women, and children, more than any savage alive, including Geronimo. I warn you, though, he does not like loud noises. So don't make a sound when you step behind this curtain. I will see if he is in a good enough mood to greet you."

It was all a ruse.

Ichabod would escort his paying customers behind the canvas wall and quietly ask the chief to say hello to the visitors. Of course, he didn't move until somebody in the crowd got tired of waiting and called out, "Turn around, ya dumb heathen!"

Then, he'd slowly get to his feet with his head bowed, cast off his black blanket, and release the most earth-shattering war cry anyone had ever heard, while threatening to leap into the crowd with a raised tomahawk and knife.

Immediately, half the crowd always fled. Those who remained were frozen with fear by his white complexion and angry pink eyes. When he growled, it always looked like he had a mouthful of blood because his gums were so red against his white skin. It was more than most city slickers could take. To Ichabod's great joy, the tiny canvas tent in which Chief White Devil presided emptied in a matter of minutes. Justice knew he had a winning show for as long as he could keep Harold sober.

* * *

OF ALL THE ACTS, Tommy and Delbert found the fortune teller and the Persian queen the most intriguing. They had gotten to know them casually because they were assigned to help set up their tent whenever the caravan stopped.

Ichabod discovered the women while wintering in Louisiana. Both had long black hair, sparkling green eyes, and wore tiny veils across their mouths. As if the veils were not enough to attract attention, both wore sparkling jewelry and brightly colored outfits that clung to their shapely figures, leaving little to the imagination.

Their names were Esmeralda and Liberty. Liberty was tall and strikingly beautiful. She danced and could swallow a sword as easily as a baby gulped milk. Esmeralda was more petite and a bit on the homely side. She had long black hair, a hooked nose, and bony fingers that went unnoticed whenever she began to tell fortunes. Together, they quickly became a favorite of Ichabod's marvelous attractions.

When he paraded them out on the stage for all to see, a sudden hush always went over the male-dominated crowd. Few men had seen two women so enchanting. Painted and catlike, their emerald eyes were so captivating that they made anyone who looked at them want to know more, especially what was behind their veils.

It cost an extra nickel to see their act too, more than any of the Marvels Ichabod regularly put on display. Esmeralda played a tiny harp as Liberty performed. When the sword swallowing concluded, Esmeralda took a seat at a tiny table, uncovered a crystal ball, and pointed to one lucky customer who would have his fortune told for free.

Her predictions or visions were uncanny. Nobody left unhappy because she always discovered some surprise within that crystal ball that would please the customer. Her statements were vague but intriguing. She would say things like:

"Your late wife says you should go west."

"Beneath a rock and next to a deep well, you will find the fortune for which you have been searching."

"Beware! Dark clouds cast shadows on your future."

Moments later, Ichabod announced private sessions with Esmeralda could be purchased for another dime. There always was a long line of fortune seekers at their tent. Liberty collected the fare with Tommy at her side. By sixteen, he was so big and intimidating, Justice used him to deter any unruly customers.

The boys' fate changed when Tommy and Delbert happened by their tent late one night. Fall had arrived, and there was a scent of damp leaves in the air. It mixed with the incense the Eastern women burned each night. A sliver moon lit up a darkened sky.

Tommy was almost seven feet tall at age sixteen. Everything about him was long—his blond hair, his legs and arms, and even his face, which was sort of horse-like. His nose hung down to his upper lip, and he had large, bulbous eyes that were as blue as a spring-fed lake on a winter day. His eyes made up for everything else. They were gorgeous. When he smiled and fluttered his eyelashes, it was hard to refuse him anything.

Shadows were long as they approached the tent, and the camp seemed extremely quiet. The tent was illuminated by a light inside, and the sounds of a struggle quickly got the boys' attention.

"What was that?" Delbert asked.

"It sounded like a cry for help," Tommy said, his eyes and ears suddenly alert. "Do you suppose it came from Esmeralda's tent?"

"Maybe someone is hurt," his friend said. "We should investigate."

"Let's go!"

Tommy was big and clumsy, but he could cover vast amounts of ground with his big stride. Del always had trouble keeping up, but he never was far behind.

When the large teen burst into the tent, he saw three cowboys wrestling with their two friends. Esmeralda was being restrained by one man, and Liberty was fending off the other two with her swords. Both were backed into far corners of the tent.

"Put the sword down, Missy," one of the thugs said. "Me and Jethro thought we might get a smooch while your friend tells Clyde over there where our chest of gold is hidden."

The three men were part of a gang of train robbers. The trio of bumbling thieves got separated from the rest of the gang during their escape and missed out on their cut of the booty. Clyde hoped the fortune teller would be able to tell him where the rest of the gang was hiding. They didn't expect such fiery resistance, though.

When Tommy happened upon the assault, he had a flashback of when his mother was attacked, kidnapped, and stolen from their tent six years earlier. He wasn't going to let it happen to his two female friends. He growled as he charged into the melee. Delbert tried to restrain him, but there was no way he could stop the determined behemoth.

Tommy charged up behind the two men Liberty was holding at bay, grabbed them by the collars of their dirty coats, and smashed their heads together. When their noggins collided, it sounded like two coconuts banging together. The thugs saw stars and collapsed onto the carpeted floor.

Liberty smiled at him and stood over the fallen

ruffians with a sword at each of their throats and said, "I've got them. Now go help Esmeralda."

Tommy towered over the small man who had cornered the fortune teller. She was screaming and clawing at him like a wildcat. With Delbert at his side, Tommy sauntered up behind the intruder and calmly tapped him on the shoulder. When he turned, Del planted an uppercut between his legs. The smell of whiskey filled the air as the man gasped and grabbed his crushed privates. That's when the big teenager delivered a second uppercut to his chin. The blow lifted the intruder off his feet. He landed hard on his back, and air rushed from his lungs.

Tommy reached his hand out to the terrified Esmeralda and said, "Are you okay? You're safe now."

"Thank you," she replied and accepted his hand, and he guided her away from her fallen attacker.

Delbert smiled wildly, placed a foot on the fallen attacker's chest, and flexed his biceps in the air as if he were the touring company's strongman.

"Hey, Tommy, we didn't do so bad. The odds were three against two, and we showed 'em who was boss. Reckon we make a pretty good team."

"You are both heroes in my book," Esmeralda said. She leaned over and brushed the tiny teen's cheek with her lips. Del was surprised and a bit enchanted. He'd never been kissed before.

With Esmeralda's attacker out cold, they turned their attention to Liberty. Her attackers were conscious but too afraid to move an inch. Tiny trickles of blood ran down their necks from where Liberty pressed the points of her swords.

"What shall we do with these brigands?" she asked without taking her eyes off the defeated outlaws.

"We didn't mean no harm," Clyde stuttered and pleaded for his life. "Let us go, and you'll never see us again."

"Why should I believe you?" Liberty asked.

"Reckon you'll have to trust me. I'm a man of my word," he replied.

"Honorable men don't barge into the tent of two women in the middle of the night," Delbert said. "What did you want?"

"We thought the fortune teller could tell us where our gold was," the other man said. When he spoke, his Adam's apple bobbed and more blood flowed.

"Please don't kill us," Clyde begged.

That's when Delbert curled his finger and motioned for the fortune teller to come closer. When she bent over, he whispered a plan in her ear.

Tommy, who weighed close to three hundred pounds, placed a foot on Clyde's stomach and said, "I think I could just squash this one if you'd like."

"No!" shouted Esmeralda. "If they promise to leave us alone, I'll tell them where they can find their gold."

Delbert smiled, and Tommy applied a little more weight on the foot that rested against Clyde's stomach. "What do you say, tough guy?" he asked.

Completely drained of oxygen, Clyde's lips moved, but no sound escaped his mouth. His face turned from red to a pale shade of blue.

"We'll do it," the other outlaw barked. "I promise."

Tommy pulled his foot away from Clyde's stomach, and the man's color returned to his face as his lungs fought for air.

Liberty looked at Esmeralda and asked, "What makes you believe such despicable men?"

"They covet the gold more than us," she replied. "By this time tomorrow, they will be far from here."

"All right. You're the one who can see into the future," Liberty said and removed the swords from their throats. With a quick flick of her wrists, she slashed the buttons from their coats and added, "If I see your ugly mugs again, I will kill you both."

"Get up slowly and go retrieve your friend," Tommy said. The man they had called Jethro was still unconscious. "Then, get out of here."

They did as they were told and rushed to their partner, helped him up, and turned to exit the tent. It was Clyde who stopped and asked, "I promise you'll never see us again. Where can we find our gold?"

"The men in your gang ride to New Orleans, where they plan to gamble with your share of the stolen cache," Esmeralda said.

"If you ride hard, you probably can catch up with them," Del said with a snicker.

The outlaws exited with smiles on their faces and promised each other they would never seek admission to another freak show as long as they lived.

In the aftermath, it was Liberty who asked the probing question of her partner. "How did you know where their gold was without consulting your crystal ball?" she queried.

"It was Delbert's idea," she replied. "I lied."

Beaming with pleasure for his fast thinking, the tiny teen explained, "New Orleans, as we all know, is far away from here. I was positive if we lied, they'd hightail it out of here, and we'd never hear from them again."

"That's pretty smart, buddy," Tommy said.

"And it was quite a punch you delivered to that man's gut too," the fortune teller said. "I don't know how we can thank you."

"How about you tell us our fortune," Delbert said.

"Yeah, that would be neat. I'd like to know where we are headed next. I don't know if I want to go to California," Tommy declared.

"I think that's a grand idea," Liberty said. "What do you think Esmeralda? I'll help you set up."

The fortune teller agreed and retrieved her crystal ball from a cabinet along with a small leather pouch. She placed it on a table in the center of the tent, and the boys took seats in chairs across from the veiled woman whose eyes sparkled in the candlelight. She placed her hands on the crystal ball. When it began to glow, it cast a soft light on all four of them. Then Esmeralda revealed what she saw.

"You boys will not go to California. Instead, you will leave the caravan and travel to Texas," she said.

"Why Texas?" Delbert asked.

"That is where you will find your parents, of course," she said. "You have been estranged from them for many years. It is time for you to be reunited."

"How do you know this?" Tommy asked, shocked by the woman's words.

"The crystal knows all. It is empowered by Isis, an ancient Egyptian god. It is she who will lead you to those you seek," the fortune teller said.

"How will we know where to look?" Delbert asked.

"Two others, an odd pair—just like you two—will assist you on your quest," the fortune teller said.

"How will we find them?" Del asked.

"This will guide you," Esmeralda said and handed Tommy the leather pouch. "Do not open it until it speaks to you."

"What's inside?" Tommy asked. "The pouch looks full but has no weight."

"Inside is a small crystal. The closer you get to Texas, the heavier your burden will become," Esmeralda mysteriously explained. "When all seems lost, the crystal will lead you to safety. Protect it with your lives, and let it guide you to a new beginning."

"We've often wondered what happened to our parents, my father, and Tommy's mother," Delbert said. "We had no idea where to begin to search. Thank you for this revelation."

"It'll be an adventure," Tommy said. "We've never been to Texas before."

Liberty leaned her head between the boys. Her perfume invaded their senses. She placed an arm around their shoulders and planted a kiss on each boy's cheek.

"Thank you for rescuing us," she said. "Now go and find the answers to the questions that have haunted you for so many years."

Esmeralda smiled at them and said warmly, "You hold your future in your hands, boys. Don't let it slip away."

Liberty handed Tommy a neatly wrapped package before the two boys left. They accepted it and left excited and somewhat speechless.

4. THE SEARCH BEGINS

TOMMY WAS WALKING FAST WHEN THEY LEFT THE WOMEN'S tent. Delbert practically had to run to keep up with him. Finally, he grabbed him by the sleeve and asked him where he was going in such a hurry.

"Weren't you listening?" he asked. "She said we could find your father and my mother in Texas."

"And you believe her?" Delbert asked.

"Yes, why would she lie?"

"I don't know. I was mesmerized by everything she said, but common sense tells me she can't really see into the future. They could be sending us on a wild goose chase."

"I don't think so. I feel completely changed by the whole experience," Tommy revealed. "When that crystal ball began to glow, I felt something change inside of me. Didn't you?"

"Now that you mention it, my mind does seem clearer," Delbert admitted. "And I feel a happiness I hadn't felt before. Maybe I'm overthinking this whole thing."

"I'm no longer the clumsy oaf I have been my entire

life," Tommy said. "My muscles are tighter, and I feel more agile. Watch this."

Tommy promptly leaped in the air and clicked his heels together. He did it right in front of his friend's face. His heels were more than three feet off the ground when he tapped them together in midair. Delbert was astonished. He had never seen Tommy's feet leave the ground since he had known him. Most of the time, he was tripping over his size eighteen clodhoppers.

Delbert stopped and stared.

"I'm stronger too," Tommy declared.

Then, he reached over, lifted his small friend off his feet, and tossed him in the air. It was as if Delbert weighed no more than a feather. Tommy spun him like a top and caught him in an instant. He was laughing when he set him back down. Delbert was dizzy and not happy.

"Don't do that again," he said angrily. "You almost made me upchuck my supper."

"Sorry, I should have warned you," Tommy said.

"Do ya think, ya big galoot?"

Suddenly, Delbert's sixth sense—the one that directs intuition—was raging. He had the uncanny feeling he and Tommy were about to embark on a grand adventure. He looked up at his friend with questioning eyes.

"So I got the feeling you're expecting me to follow you to Texas no matter what. Is that right?" he asked.

"Yes, of course!" Tommy said and resumed his long stride.

Again, Delbert stopped and grabbed him by the sleeve. When he turned to him, he said, "Are you serious?"

"Yes! We are going to go find M. Once we find her, we will find your father. Wouldn't you like to meet that man who brought you into this world?"

"Yes, but how will you know where to look? Texas is a big place."

"Esmeralda said the crystal in the pouch would guide us when we get there," Tommy added.

"Right! An ancient god of some sort will speak to us. Do you really believe that?" Del asked and shook his head skeptically.

"Yes, I heard a voice that assured me we would find what we seek, namely our parents," the tall teen explained.

"And what did this voice say?"

"It said our troubles would come to an end when we got to Texas and found our parents," Tommy said.

"And you believe this?"

"Yes."

"How are we going to get there?" the diminutive one asked.

"Liberty is giving us a horse and a mule because they are not going on to California with Ichabod. She said they plan to join a wagon train and travel to the New Mexico Territory."

"Again, how will we know where to look when we get to Texas?" Delbert asked.

"The voice said we will receive guidance along the way," Tommy said.

"From whom?"

"I don't know, but I trust you and whatever is in this leather bag," Tommy said. "You are smarter than you realize, and you will find the way to Texas. Del, unlike me, you seldom make errors in judgment. I can't do this without you. Together, we're going to find our parents."

Delbert smiled because his friend had never complimented him before. He thought maybe the crystal ball had created some change in the big oaf. Regardless, it was nice knowing someone valued his judgment. Slowly, he was beginning to see their quest in a different light.

"That's the nicest thing you've ever said to me," Delbert said. "Maybe the crystal has changed both of us so we can endure this new journey. Just make sure you tuck the leather pouch somewhere safe. Remember, Esmeralda said to guard it with your life."

"It's in my pocket and never will leave my side," Tommy assured.

"Let's do it then," Del said with confidence.

After saying goodbye to a tearful Miss Hutchins and collecting the last of their pay from Ichabod, the teenagers headed south toward Texas.

* * *

WHEN THE ODD duo made their first night camp, Delbert tended to the campfire and cooking, while Tommy cared for the animals. Weary from a full day of riding, the teens were staring into the flames as they waited for biscuits to bake. The aroma of bacon frying over the open flames made their mouths water because they hadn't eaten all day.

Suddenly, Tommy sat up straight and tilted his head slightly as if he heard a noise in the distance. Delbert saw his reaction and immediately asked, "What's wrong, Tommy?"

Tommy held up one finger as if to hush him for a moment and then said, "You're not going to believe this. A voice just whispered in my ear."

"What do you mean?" Delbert asked.

"Just as I said. It sounded like Esmeralda was talking to me," his tall friend explained.

"Yeah, and the moon is made of green cheese too."

Tommy gave his friend a caustic look, got up, and walked to where their gear was piled. He grabbed a saddlebag and returned to the fire.

"What? Do you have something else you want me to cook?" Delbert asked.

"No. Esmeralda said danger is near, and we should arm ourselves."

"Neither of us owns a gun," Delbert said with a worried look on his face. "How stupid were we to start this journey without a firearm?"

"She said we should look in the package they gave us when we left their tent two nights ago."

"I forgot all about it," Delbert said. "What was in it?"

"I suspected it was food, packed it away, and forgot about it," Tommy replied as he pulled the tightly wrapped package from the saddlebag. When he untied the strings and unfolded the brown paper, he found a holster, a Colt revolver, a small señorita pistol, and another small leather bag.

"That bag looks exactly like the one that held the crystal she gave us," Delbert said.

Immediately, Tommy reached into his pocket, pulled out the bag with the crystal, and flashed it before his friend so there would be no confusion.

"This new bag has some weight to it," he said. "I'll bet it's extra bullets for these pistols." He handed Del the bag with the crystal inside and opened the new one. His intuition was right. It was filled with bullets.

Delbert was less interested in the artillery than he was in the mysterious contents of the bag he held. He opened it and reached inside. Then he grasped it in his right hand and pulled it out. Instantly, the tiny ball began to exude heat and a yellowish glow. He dropped it and said, "What in tarnation?"

His eyes were as big as saucers, and Tommy looked at him oddly.

"I don't know," replied Tommy. "It looks a lot like that crystal ball Esmeralda used to tell our fortune. It's much smaller, though."

Tommy didn't hesitate. He picked the ball up so he could examine it. Immediately, his fingers wrapped around it, and his entire hand began to glow yellow. Tommy's eyes grew wide, and his lips trembled. Del became worried and wrenched the crystal ball from his hand and placed it back in the leather bag.

"What did that thing do to you?" he asked as Tommy came out of what appeared to be a trance-like state.

"As you said, it was warm in my hand, but the voice spoke to me again. It said we should prepare to defend ourselves."

"What the hell does that mean?" Delbert asked.

"I think it means those women are looking out for us," Tommy said as he reached for the firearms. Tommy handed his friend the derringer and then stood and strapped the holster around his waist. It fit him perfectly and he reveled in the feeling of security it gave him. He pulled the pistol from the holster a couple of times, spun it on his finger, and slammed it back into the black holster.

"How did you do that?" Delbert asked, astonished by his friend's dexterity.

"Before M disappeared, she had Billy Tango show me how to handle a pistol," Tommy said.

"Do you mean Billy Tango, the sharpshooter? He spent a summer with the touring company some time ago," Del said.

"Yep!"

"So you know how to shoot that thing?"

"Yep!"

"Good, because trouble just arrived," Delbert said and nodded toward the area where the horse and mule were hobbled.

When Tommy turned to look, a dusty cowboy had his pistol drawn and pointed right at them.

"Oh shit!" Delbert muttered under his breath.

"Now, you can unbuckle that gun belt and let it fall to the ground, big guy," the cowboy snarled.

Tommy was shocked. He froze for a minute and thought about drawing on the intruder, but decided against it when the cowboy fired a bullet into the dirt at his feet.

He did as he was told.

Meanwhile, Delbert slipped the tiny derringer into his coat pocket and never took his eyes off the intruder.

"We don't want any trouble, mister," he said. "What do you want from us?"

The cowboy laughed and said, "I want your money, of course, ya freak."

By age sixteen, Delbert was an inch shy of four feet tall with his boots on. He took a deep breath as he seethed inside.

"We ain't got no money," Tommy replied and gave Del a quick look of confidence.

"In that case, I'll just take your holster and your horses. I'll be able to trade them for real cash at the trading post down the way," he said as he walked toward the two teens. He motioned for Tommy to step away from the pistol.

As he bent down to retrieve Tommy's holster, he added, "You two are the oddest pair I've ever seen. You ever think about joining one of those traveling sideshows?"

Delbert was still sitting next to the fire, and the man's comments made his blood boil. He reached into his coat pocket, wrapped his fingers around the derringer, and said, "Has anybody ever told you, you're dumber than dirt?"

The comment caught the cowboy by surprise. His fingers had just grasped the holster when Delbert sassed him. He turned with anger toward the tiny teen and got the biggest surprise of his life.

Smiling like he didn't have a care in the world, Delbert had the tiny pistol pointed straight at the cowboy. When he pulled the trigger at point-blank range, the .22-caliber bullet entered the cowboy's left eye, rattled around in his brain for a couple of seconds, and catapulted him onto his back. His body twitched a couple of times as Tommy looked down at him. Then, he was gone.

"Hot damn!" Tommy said. "Where'd you learn to shoot like that?"

"Never shot a gun in my life," Delbert said. "But it wasn't too hard to figure out. He was so close, there was no way I could miss him. I'm just glad the women decided to load it before they wrapped it up."

"You reckon we're going to be under attack this whole trip?" Tommy asked.

"I have no idea," Delbert said. "You'd better check with Esmeralda on that one."

"How do you expect me to check..." Tommy started and paused. "Oh, yeah. I'm going to have to thank her too."

"How do the two of you communicate?" Delbert asked.

"I haven't got the slightest idea. It happens all of a sudden, and I can hear her voice in my brain. She understands when I have questions too."

"I thought that whole crystal ball thing was one of Ichabod's hair-brained tricks, but there must be something to it," Delbert said.

"I'm glad it ain't a ruse," Tommy said. "It saved our bacon."

"Not hardly," Delbert said. "The bacon's burned and so are the biscuits."

"It makes no difference to me. I'm as hungry as a bear," Tommy said.

"Well, let's eat and get out of here as soon as we can. If I have to look at that dead cowboy for very long, I'm going to lose my appetite."

5. COLD REALITY

Somewhere in West Texas...

AFTER THEIR ENCOUNTER WITH THE WOULD-BE ROBBER, the teens made a mad dash for Texas. Delbert mounted the cowboy's mustang so they could make better time. All their gear was placed on the mule so they could travel with greater speed. The terrain they were accustomed to changed suddenly as Texas grew near. Gone were the tall prairie grasses. Mesquite and cacti graced the horizon. Tommy saw the mountains ahead, where cottonwoods grew in abundance.

Delbert hadn't been paying much attention to what direction they were riding. The reality of taking the cowboy's life had suddenly set in. He had never before seen a dead man, let alone been the cause of another man's demise. It tormented him to the point of distraction.

When they stopped to rest their horses, Tommy took the opportunity to inquire why his partner had been so quiet. "You haven't said a word all day." Tommy asked, "What's going on with you?"

"Nothing!" he replied shortly.

"I know better than that," his friend added. "It's not like you to be so quiet. Do you want to head back to the touring troupe?"

"No."

"Then talk to me, or I'm turning back and abandoning this search. I'm not so sure this isn't a wild goose chase anyway."

"Don't do that just yet. I'm trying to get my head around the fact I killed a man back there," Delbert admitted.

"He most certainly was going to harm us. I don't know if he was going to kill us, but we would have been as good as dead if he had walked off with all our belongings. If you haven't noticed, it's getting mighty cold."

"Does that justify what I did?" Delbert asked.

"In my book, it does. You not only saved your own life, but you saved mine. So thank you." Tommy said.

"For some reason, that doesn't make me feel any better," Delbert said. "I keep replaying the whole incident in my head. Over and over, I see that cowboy's eye explode. It's haunting me."

Tommy reached into his pocket for the leather pouch the exotic woman had given them. He ordered Delbert to hold out his hand. When he did, he dumped the ball into his open palm.

"What's this for?" Delbert asked.

"Give it a few seconds and you will know," his friend replied.

Without realizing it, Delbert's small fingers grasped the ball. Unlike Tommy, whose hands were four times larger, half the ball remained above his fingertips. When it began to glow, Delbert's eyes widened, and his lips began to move, but no sound was emitted.

He was motionless when a soft voice began to speak to him. "Where you go, death will follow. You must learn to take a stand if you wish to survive. The señorita pistol is small, like you, but it evens the odds. Your enemies won't suspect it. Fear not what you do. Fear what you fail to do. Now go. Find your destiny."

When he let the crystal ball slip from his fingers, Tommy caught it in both of his massive palms and returned it to the leather pouch. A calmness washed over Delbert's being. His anxiety disappeared, and he felt refreshed.

"How do you feel now?" Tommy asked.

"Remarkable!"

"Do we return to Ichabod's caravan, or do we continue on our quest?" Tommy asked.

"We've come too far to turn back now," Delbert said. "The temperature is dropping, and we have a few hours before the sun goes down. Let's continue south. In a few hours, we'll be in Texas."

"How do you know that?" his partner asked.

"I don't know. Call it intuition," Delbert said, and grabbed the reins of the mustang. "Let's get moving."

"Where to?" Tommy asked.

"This is unfamiliar territory. We will find refuge in the mountains."

"What makes you say that?" Tommy asked.

"I don't know. My intuition seems very strong now."

* * *

THE BOYS COULD SEE the Guadalupe Mountain range in the distance. It was on the horizon but still far away. Delbert estimated they might reach them in a couple of days because they were moving at a slow, relaxed pace. There was no reason to hurry and put additional strain on the animals.

Suddenly, they heard a clamor coming from behind them. When they turned, they saw two men, clad in buckskin, riding toward them at great speed. They were shouting and raising long rifles over their heads.

"This looks like trouble," Tommy said. "Are they shouting at us?"

"I'm not sure," Del said. "They are too far away to make out their words completely. Let's see what they want."

With that, the boys turned their horses toward the men and waited for them to get closer. They didn't have to wait long. The riders were closing the distance with great speed. Dust kicked up behind the two giant horses, and both men were leaning into their mounts, urging them forward.

When they shouted again, the boys understood their words clearly, and they froze in place for several seconds.

"Run! Indian war party!" the lead rider called out. He wore a coonskin cap and had a wild look in his eyes when he reined in his Appaloosa next to the boys. Their horses were huffing hard and stamping their hooves when the other man pulled to a stop alongside Tommy.

"Did you hear what we said, boy?" the man shouted excitedly. "There's a war party on our heels. They are a mile back. If you don't get a move on it, you're gonna die."

They didn't wait for an answer. Both men booted their horses forward and continued their run toward the mountains.

"Where are you running to?" Tommy called out just as he sped off.

"Texas, God willin'!" he shouted.

"Us too," said Delbert. He looked at his best friend with fear in his eyes and said, "Let's go, Tommy. That dust cloud on the horizon has to be Indians. We've come too far to die when we're this close to Texas."

"I don't want to die ever," his big partner said and booted his horse forward at full speed. Delbert dug his heels into his mount and tried to catch up with his partner.

They rode hard for thirty minutes, but it felt more like thirty hours to the boys, whose backsides were not accustomed to riding horses on the run.

When they got to a gulch, they found the two buck-skin-clad men waiting for them. They had their rifles resting on boulders because they had given up running from the war party.

Tommy reined the mustang. It skidded to a stop just past the two men and the boulders they leaned against. He spun the mare around to where the two Indian fighters planned to make a stand and asked, "What'd you stop for?"

"Our horses are plumb tuckered out," the tall man replied with a determined look in his eye. "We figured to make a stand here. Maybe ambush them and trim their numbers some."

The man looked like he had just come down from the mountains. He wore all leather and had moccasin boots that laced to his knees. He was sweating and his long black hair was sticking to his neck and face, which was covered with gray stubble.

His partner was short and stout. He was dressed identically but wore a long beard and mustache. His brown hair was tied in pigtails. When he took off his blue cavalry hat to wipe sweat from his brow, he had an ugly scar across the top of his head where hair once had been.

"Why are they chasing you?" Tommy asked.

"You're an odd-looking pair and must be greener than the Kansas Prairie," the tall one said. "We're White men, and this is Indian land."

"It is?" Tommy asked. "Do you mean we're trespassing?"

"Too Tall and Too Small here must be Easterners," the short man said. "You best hightail it out of here. We'll hold 'em off. I doubt you men will make it halfway to Texas, though. There are more Indians and rough country ahead."

Delbert didn't like the sound of that.

"What do the Indians want?" he asked as the tall man reached up and grabbed the halter of his horse to keep it from prancing.

"They want our rifles, our food, and our horses," the stranger said.

"They love scalps too," the short man said with a loud snicker. "They took a patch of mine a few years ago, but it ain't gonna happen again." He took off his hat and pointed to the ugly scar on the crown of his head.

"They gonna love your hair, though" he added and chuckled again.

"We got a rifle and some food on our mule," Delbert

said. "Do you think if we left it for them, they might stop chasing us?"

The two old-timers looked at each other as if the boy had declared the world was flat and they were about to ride off the edge.

"That just might work," the tall one said. "At least it'll slow them down for a while and give us a chance to skedaddle."

"Make sure there ain't no bullets in that rifle, men. An empty rifle can't kill nobody," the other one said as he climbed back onto his saddle and prepared to ride off.

Tommy and the tall stranger tied the mule to a tree alongside the trail and then jumped back onto their horses and rode off at breakneck speed again.

The deceptive tactic worked. The riders had put ten miles between them and the site where they intended to ambush the Indians. The mule and the goods they left behind obviously appeased the Indians because the dust cloud that pursued them no longer existed.

They slowed their tired horses to a canter. Everyone was breathing heavily, especially Tommy and Delbert, who were not used to riding at such a furious pace.

The tall stranger rode up next to Delbert and proudly introduced himself.

"I'm Claud Fisher, and that there is Smitty," he said. "That was darn quick thinking to leave that mule behind. Thank you for doing that."

"Quite a sacrifice too," Smitty added.

"But it worked. Texas ain't far off now. We might make it home by Christmas after all, Smitty," Fisher said.

"Where y'all headin'?" Smitty asked.

"Like you, Texas!" Delbert said.

"You're welcome to ride with us," Fisher said. "Will get you to the mountains there. Then we're going to head off to Colorado City.

"You men should be safe from the Indians there," Smitty added. "Just keep an eye on your back trail, and be alert all the time."

"How far off is that?" Tommy asked.

"We'll need to rest our horses here, but we can be there in a few hours," Fisher said.

"I feel the temperature droppin', Claude. While we give these animals a blow, I'll make some coffee. It's going to be a chilly night," Smitty said.

Over coffee, the men explained they had not been home for a couple of years. They had given up all hope of finding gold in the northern high country and were eager to get back to Texas. Tommy and Delbert told them about their quest to find their parents. Neither man had heard of Emily Turnbolt or Jack Elliott. The hot coffee was refreshing, though. They finished up and headed back out onto the trail.

They split up at the foot of the mountains and bid each other farewell. Again, the hunters thanked Tommy and Del for their fast thinking and said they were welcome at their campfire if they ever got to Colorado City.

Tommy and Delbert were sorry they had lost their mule and supplies, but were happy they had made new friends.

There was one thing the hunters did that agreed with the boys more than anything else.

"They treated us like men, not boys," Delbert observed. "That sure felt good, didn't it, Tommy?"

"Yep, I think we're going to like Texas."

* * *

BY THE TIME they reached the mountains, the sun was sinking into the western horizon. A clear, blue sky gave way to the grayness that heralded the arrival of the moon and the stars. The air was crisp. Plumes of steam escaped from the noses of the horses, which were beginning to labor in the thinner air.

"We need to find water for these horses," Tommy said. "They are breathing pretty heavy."

"Yes, and we need to find a cave to protect us from the cold and lots of wood for a fire. My feet and hands are freezing," said Delbert, his teeth chattering slightly from the cold. The temperature had dropped at least twenty degrees.

Both the teens had pulled on their winter coats and had blankets wrapped around their shoulders and over their heads. It wasn't enough to fend off the coldest temperatures Texas had seen in decades.

"Something tells me we'll find water just ahead," Del said. "There is an unusual amount of green vegetation on the edge of that next rise. It's getting water from somewhere. Let's go find out."

The closer they got to the oasis, the faster the horses began to move. They could smell the water and green grass. Delbert let his reins go and allowed his mustang to lead the duo to where they would camp for the night.

When a tiny pool of water appeared, surrounded by a dozen or more cottonwoods, Tommy was shocked.

"Dadgumit, that intuition of yours is becoming as

reliable as Molly, Miss Hutchins's dairy cow," he said. "What's going on?"

"I have no idea," Delbert said. "All I remember is Esmeralda telling us we would find our way once we got to Texas. I reckon that's what we're doin'."

Del's mustang tapped at a thin coating of ice atop the water and lowered its head to drink.

"That mustang sure acts like he knows what he's doing," Tommy said. "Maybe he's been here before."

"I don't know, but I don't like the fact it's cold enough for a thin layer of ice to form on that water. We're in for a cold night, and we'd better get a fire going. You take care of the animals, and I'll gather some kindling to start a fire."

A steady breeze kicked up as Delbert got his campfire started. His eyes tingled, and his nose dripped. He was chilled to the bone, and the fire didn't seem to be helping him warm up.

After hobbling the animals where they could eat and drink their fill, Tommy strolled to the fire and stamped his feet to get them warm. His hands were cold, and he stretched them over the fire for warmth. It didn't work very well. The campfire was too small.

"We need some larger timbers for this fire," he said and went in search of something that would burn hotter. He didn't find much because they were camped on the side of a mountain.

When he returned, Delbert was physically shaking beneath his winter coat and blanket.

"I-If hell f-freezes o-over, this is w-what it is going to f-feel like," he chattered.

Tommy immediately sat behind his friend and wrapped him in his massive arms. "Let my body heat warm you a little," he said. "Then we have to find shelter or we're going to freeze to death out here."

"I g-got an i-idea," Delbert said. "G-Get c-crystal b-ball. W-warm."

"Why didn't I think about that," Tommy said, and he retrieved the leather pouch from his pocket. "Can you open your hands?" he asked.

"T-Trying," his partner said.

Tommy placed the orb between Delbert's palms and wrapped his fingers around it. Then he draped his own mammoth hands around those of Delbert. The orb began to glow and exude a small amount of heat. Immediately, their hands began to tingle as the blood began to flow again and heat spread through their fingers.

"That feels wonderful," Delbert said. "And I think help is on the way."

"What do you mean by help?" Tommy asked.

"Not sure. Again, my intuition is strong," Delbert replied.

6. POTAK'S ALLY

In a secluded cave in Seminole Canyon, Texas

AS THE TONKAWA WARRIOR WAITED BEFORE THE ROARING fire, the medicine man reached into his pouch and pulled out his worn corncob pipe. He used his warming fingers to fumble it open and fill the bowl with a potent mix of herbs. He used the flat of his knife to select a fiery cinder of just the right size, and he placed it in the middle of the bowl and puffed it to life. In seconds smoke swirled around his head, blurring his face. His eyes quickly sparkled in the firelight when he passed the pipe to his cousin. Tuc also took a long drag of the magic potion. He held it deep in his lungs for a moment before expulsing a thick, gray cloud.

The bats grew irritated from the sweet, pungent smell of the shaman's herbal mix and the smoke from the fire, which rose with the heat. The room shone so brightly from the Indians' bonfire, it was more than the free-tailed bats could tolerate. Soon they could endure no more. Suddenly, they all took flight, and the black mass fled out of the cave's entrance. The stream of flying bats was so dense it looked like one long snake as it writhed its way from the shelter and into the freezing night. For a moment, the entrance was completely blocked out by the dark mass of flittering wings.

"This could be a sign and part of my vision," Potak whispered. "It is not normal for bats to fly out into such bad weather."

"Maybe they didn't like the smoke." Tuc snickered, believing the obvious. But Potak paid him no mind—he knew better.

The shaman's eyes were now glassy, and he smiled. The apparent discomfort from the freezing snowstorm now seemed to be forgotten as his movements became less mechanical and his mind traveled to a more pleasant place. Tuc watched his cousin in awe as his physical appearance changed. Tuc knew himself as among the fiercest warriors in Texas and northern Mexico. But he begrudgingly had to admit his cousin possessed something so much more powerful. He, at times, felt weak in the face of a man who could travel across the dimensions at will and feel no fear of the darkness and extreme unknown. Potak's body suffered from age, but his mind relished in the knowledge acquired from his time on earth.

The bats' wings were like four-fingered hands. A thin membrane of skin covered the bones creating their flexible wings. Potak knew these finger-like bones gave them the skill to change direction in an instant. They fled out of the cave entrance at nearly a hundred miles an hour—their maximum speed. Mexican free-tailed bats were common in the southern United States and northern Mexico.

Unknown to the local natives, the scientific name for the bat came from the Greek word *cheir*, which means hand, and *pteron*, meaning wing. The bats had a thin layer of black and gray fur with small ears and black beady eyes. Some weighed as little as a penny, while others could be as heavy as a brick.

Bats were mythical creatures for the North American tribes. In native folklore, bats are believed to be trapped between the lives of birds and mammals and were rejected by both groups. However, they would occasionally act as spies or traitors for the Indian spirits. Potak knew sometimes bats played the role of tricksters. Some tribes, like the Blackfoot, thought they were poison. Others thought they fed on people. The Tonkawa medicine man had studied bats for years and knew that most beliefs were unfounded and generally tall tales. Regardless of their questionable position in the natural world, all Indians knew bats could predict the weather. Today, however, their flight indicated confusion.

Maybe I should reconsider the value of bats and spirits, Potak thought to himself as he watched them flee into the storm.

This was not an everyday occurrence, regardless of the fire. These mammals knew more about the weather than any animals on earth. Perhaps someone else is coming they don't dare encounter. The cousins looked at each other and questioned the odd behavior. When the last bat flew out into the blizzard, the only sound was that of the crackling fire and humans breathing.

"I believe we will have visitors," Potak said after an hour of silence. He needed time to evaluate what they had witnessed.

Tuc began to snicker and said, "And where do you think visitors will come from when we are hidden here in a cave in the middle of a snowstorm? Anyone out there tonight will freeze to death."

"I can only tell you what I read in the signs," Potak said confidently.

The flames made the cave come alive with shadows that slithered like snakes off the walls and ceiling. Warm waves of air flowed through the cave despite the freezing temperature outside. The old medicine man rubbed his hands together and then opened his palms. He placed them as close to the fire as he dared. After he was thoroughly warm, he removed a pot and began to prepare black beans with salted pork.

"Why are you making so much food?" Tuc asked. "We can't eat that much."

"I told you. I am expecting guests," Potak said. "We are in the solstice. It is time to show friendship and hospitality. We can provide the gift of warmth and food for our visitors."

Tuc just laughed at the idea of somebody showing up in such a difficult place. But he knew better than to argue with his cousin, no matter how crazy his idea was. Although they often amounted to nothing, his visions many times were essential to their survival. Even though he scoffed somewhere in the back of his mind, he didn't altogether reject the possibility. Over the years of travel with his shaman cousin, he had come to believe most all things were possible. If it was imaginable, then it could come to be. But his urge to complain or to be ornery was irresistible.

"Next, you'll be telling me you believe in Christmas like the White men," Tuc chided.

"Never reject a belief shared by so many people," Potak warned. "Just because it is not our way does not mean it isn't dangerous to dismiss. I believe there are many ways to believe in the same thing, and there are many names for the same god. How could only the Native American Indians be right in their beliefs? Is the rest of the world wrong? It is a fool who thinks only they are right, and the rest of the world is ignorant."

Tuc wanted to protest even more, but he couldn't find a sound reason. Deep down inside, the Tonkawa warrior believed most of the things his cousin had taught him. He knew his power as a warrior, in part, was due to his cousin's knowledge, although he would never admit the same to Potak. That would be more than his pride could withstand.

The cold made them hungrier than usual, and the hot beans and salty pork warmed them from the inside out. As the wind howled just outside, both Indians enjoyed the warmth of the fire and the protection of the cave. Tuc was even beginning to enjoy it. He ventured to the entrance, and the wind immediately hit him. The scalps that were sewn to his buckskins fluttered as though they would escape and disappear into the howling gusts. Snowflakes as big as a man's thumb fell by the millions. Tuc had removed his moccasins beside the fire and now stood barefoot, ankle-deep in the white powder. He felt the cold crawl up his legs. As his gaze attempted to pierce the night, a nearly full moon gave a silver cast of light across the canyon and its walls.

His eyes narrowed and his brow furrowed. Tuc thought he saw something move out in the night. It disappeared in the whiteness of the storm. With hawk-like eyes, he scanned the area where he saw movement.

Then, he saw it again, but now it appeared to be two images—one large and one small like a little bear. Finally, the silhouettes contrasted with the white stone walls behind them. It was a tall man whose shadow was enormous. He was accompanied by a tiny person less than a third of his stature. The second shadow was more like that of a child.

They both were huddled next to a small fire. That was when Tuc looked behind him and noted the bright glow of the fire that illuminated the entrance to the cave. He imagined it looked like a giant eye of light from out in the stormy night. He grumbled as he recalled what his cousin had said. As unlikely as it seemed, two people were pointing to the path the Tonkawa had climbed to the cave. Tuc grimaced again. He knew the strangers had spotted their cave and soon would climb the path to seek refuge. He was not in the mood to tolerate two unknown fools or to admit to his cousin he was once again correct.

"Potak," Tuc cried out above the howling wind. "You better come out here and have a look at this."

When Potak looked down at the base of the mountain, he saw the silhouettes of the two strangers next to a small campfire. They were immersed in an unusual amount of light. The large man's hands seemed to glow.

"Crazy White men. They'll never survive in this weather," the fierce warrior said.

"We must help him," Potak said.

"Why?"

"There is something strange about this man," Potak said as he inhaled his pipe and released a long stream of fragrant smoke. "Plus, he has a child with him."

"Really? What is so strange about a White man and a child on a cold Texas night?"

"Look, he captures light. Have you ever seen a campfire that small give off so much light?"

"You are imagining things that are not obvious to me, cousin. Perhaps the smoke and cold are affecting your reasoning," Tuc countered, but didn't want to argue. It was too cold.

"You should know by now the universe is full of magical things," Potak said.

"I have never seen White man's magic," Tuc said.

"I am curious and want to learn more. You may stay here or join me."

7. SYMPATHY AND UNDERSTANDING

In a secluded cave in Seminole Canyon, Texas

As reluctant as Tuc was to follow his cousin on yet another wild goose chase, he would not let him venture into the unknown alone. Since they did not know what sort of men they would confront, they moved from shadow to shadow like two apparitions floating across the night. With the magic of smoke flowing through Potak's veins, he no longer felt the cold, and his instincts became enhanced. Both men saw the intruders were armed so they approached with more caution than if they were simple souls lost in the wilderness. The more Potak observed the glowing fire—the more intrigued he grew. What they had thought to be a small fire turned out to be some strange object in the stranger's hands. The amount of light it provided was intense, almost as great as the fire the Tonkawa had built in the cave to keep them warm.

The Tonkawa realized immediately the huddled mass was not a father and child but two young boys, perhaps brothers. One was gargantuan, the other was tiny.

"What are you two boys doing out here in a blizzard?" Potak asked as he whispered in their ears.

As soon as the shaman spoke, the two boys were awakened. Tommy reached for his pistol and Delbert, startled badly, almost dropped the tiny ball of light. It glowed with such intensity Potak had to squint to protect his eyes from its brightness. The small campfire cast a faint orange glow; the ball radiated a golden light, much like the sun.

Tuc placed his knife against the large boy's throat and whispered, "We mean you no harm. If you choose violence, you will die."

Tommy tensed and looked from one Indian to the other and asked, "What do you want? We have no money."

"You have nothing we want," Potak said, "but we have shelter, something you require. We have a dry and warm place to stay, and it is not far," Potak said as he pointed to the entrance of the cave that glowed orange above their heads. "You must come with us, or you will perish out here in the storm."

Potak smiled warmly, wrinkles rippling across his cheeks. The other Indian's face glared in angry indifference. His eyes seemed to radiate evil in the golden light. Indecision rested heavily on the boys' minds as snow accumulated on the blankets that covered their shoulders. Potak was transfixed by the light coming from the small boy's hands. He wanted to know more about the White man's magic. He had never seen anything so curious before.

"Come," Potak repeated. "What have you got to lose?

If you stay here, the storm will blow your small fire away and you both will freeze to death."

"Heed my cousin's warning," Tuc whispered in the large boy's ear. "The storm has not reached its full strength yet."

Tommy and Delbert still were hesitant to comply with the invitation of the strange-looking man, although they both realized what they said of the storm was probably true. The blizzard had increased in strength for the entire day and showed no signs of letting up. Delbert looked up at the moon but the freezing haze and snow all but blocked it from his sight. Was this what the crystal ball had warned of or was this part of their new and mysterious destiny?

"Tommy, we must go with them," Del said, but his giant of a friend didn't budge.

The crystal ball grew even brighter in Tommy's hands. Tommy tilted his head to one side like he was listening to a voice. When the glowing mass became so bright they all had to squint.

"I feel it is safe," Del added.

"Yes, the crystal says these men mean us no harm," Tommy added.

Potak's eyebrows raised as the odd White boys became more curious. Were they hearing voices?

As soon as the words escaped Tommy's lips, the intense light dimmed and then went out. Without the warmth it spread, the boys' teeth began to chatter. Their eyes spread wide when Tuc suddenly appeared next to the gentle-looking Indian. He scowled and gripped his Bowie tightly in his hand. The boys gasped. He reminded them of the savagery and hatred that existed between the two races, neither of which they had experienced. They were familiar with the dime novels that depicted the Indians' heinous acts against White settlers.

Potak chuckled and said, "Do not be afraid of my cousin. He likes to scare White people, especially green boys who are new to the Texas wilderness. I promise you no harm. We have a warm cave close by where we all will be safe from the storm. We just have to climb this path. But we must hurry. When the storm is upon us, there will be a whiteout and then none of us will have a chance to reach safety. Come along. Perhaps when you get comfortable, you will tell me of this object that shines so brightly."

Both Tommy and Del looked momentarily from the Indians to the white curtain of weather that was heading their way. It was a solid wall of snow that could not be penetrated by the human eye. If they decided to stay, it was clear they would not survive. Their only chance was to trust the crystal ball and the word of the leathery old Indian. Perhaps the ball guided them to this spot so they could be rescued.

Without a word, Tuc turned and began the steep climb up the path to the cave and Potak followed. Delbert scrambled behind the medicine man and Tommy followed pushing his small friend before him as they clawed their way to a landing halfway up the canyon wall. Tuc quickly scaled the path as his cousin struggled some. The boys slipped on occasion, but their youthful agility and desire for warmth kept them moving upward.

As soon as they stepped into the large cave the force of the fierce wind disappeared, although it still howled like a forlorn beast in the darkness. The snow at the entrance was more than a foot deep and large drifts began to appear across the canyon floor. In minutes the blizzard was on them, and visibility dropped to zero. The whiteout had arrived, and they were in the eye of the storm.

"Do you now see that you made the right choice? Safety always is the best choice." Potak chuckled. "Had you stayed where you were, you would not have survived more than an hour or two."

"How did you know we were out there?" Del asked.

"I had a vision." Potak smiled. "My ally is smoke, and it told me we would have visitors. We came here for a vision that would guide us to our future."

"Did your vision tell you about the storm?" Tommy asked doubtfully.

"My cousin sees many things normal people don't see," Tuc said, scaring the two boys even more. Then he forced a smile which only made him more frightening. Potak placed a hand on each of the young man's shoulders and calmed their souls with kind eyes. "Don't you think if we planned to harm you, we would have done so already?" he whispered.

"So, why have you helped us?" Del asked.

"Because we both have secrets to share," Potak whispered in a voice so low they could hardly hear it over the howling wind. "You possess a magic ball, and we can help you find that which you seek. This is the time of the winter solstice. So, it is time to help one another."

"It is December. What is the winter solstice? We have not heard of that before," Tommy said.

"It is a time when all things in the universe retreat. The sun dims its light so Mother Earth can sleep. When she awakens, we hope she will provide great gifts."

"How did you know we were looking for something?" Tommy asked defensively. He still was not sure of the Indians' intentions.

"Potak is a famous medicine man," Tuc said. "He speaks with our Tonkawa spirits, and they tell him many things."

White Devil, the Indian who accompanied the touring company, was actually a White man. So, neither Del nor Tommy had experience in dealing or conversing with Indians. The reality was much scarier than they had anticipated, but the old man wrapped in blankets had kind eyes. The odd friends had a good feeling about him. The tall warrior they were not so sure about. He still scared them.

"I have made food for us all," Potak said as he provided Tommy and Delbert tin pie pans which he filled with bean stew and salted pork. "Here. This will help you regain your warmth."

"How did you know to make food for visitors?" Del asked. He was one of the smallest humans the Tonkawa had ever seen but he seemed to be less scared than his large partner. Their sizes were so extremely different it made them almost a comical duo. Potak chuckled some more.

"Here is some hot coffee," he added. "It will warm your cold hands and your bellies."

When Tommy and Del tried the thick, strong java, the bitter taste contorted their faces. But it did warm their hands, and they felt the heat run down their throats and warm their stomachs. Slowly their teeth stopped chattering and their bodies stopped trembling.

"Would you like more to eat?" Potak asked as the two boys wiped their pie pans clean with hard bread from days before. For the pair, it was some of the best food they had ever eaten in days, almost like a Christmas feast. Tommy and Delbert vigorously nodded their heads, and Potak added two more spoonsful to each pan. He continued to snicker and chuckle as they wolfed down the second helping faster than the first. Tuc's face remained chiseled in stone. He didn't like White men in general and had even less patience for young greenhorns fresh from the east.

After their huge meal, Potak gave each boy a slice of hard tack to chew on as he watched them with keen interest.

"Ask them," Tuc said. "What are you waiting for?"

Both boys looked toward Tuc. Then their eyes drifted to the medicine man questioningly.

"What do you want to ask us?" Del asked with raised eyebrows.

"We are curious about the magic ball," Potak whispered almost reverently. "I have never seen such an object. Would you let me touch it?"

Del looked at Tommy, who shrugged. Then, he added, "They did save us from the blizzard."

Tommy nodded his head, and he handed the pouch and ball to the old man with thin, leathery fingers. The ancient Tonkawa's eyes lit up like stars as he held the leather pouch in his hands. He pulled the string that tied it closed and opened the top. He stared inside and expected the light of the orb to blind him. Instead, it seemed dull and lifeless. When he had seen it before, it appeared to be like a star, bright and shiny; it was full of life.

Potak let it roll into his palm and carefully wrapped his long, spindly fingers around the perfectly round piece of glass. He was surprised by its weightlessness. He stretched his bony fingers around it like a spider's web around a fly, but it remained lifeless and dull. It appeared just like any other piece of glass he had ever seen. He cast a puzzled look at the boys.

"Why does it not glow?" Potak asked, bewildered.

"I don't know," Del replied as he stared on. He also was confused.

"Where did you find this?" Potak asked, now more interested than ever.

"We think it is a crystal," Tommy said. "Esmeralda had one that was three times larger. She used it in her act for the Marvelous Marvels Touring Company."

The medicine man's eyebrows raised and he looked at his cousin without grinning. They could communicate without speaking. The boys had captured his interest.

Potak was aware certain stones evoked great spirits and could affect the human condition. By keeping crystals, Native Americans believed they gained a natural rhythm with the earth.

"Who is the person who gave you the ball?" the medicine man asked.

"She is a fortune teller. She and Liberty, an Egyptian princess, were part of the touring company we were part of before we came to Texas," Del replied.

"Witches?" Tuc whispered.

"It is dark magic," Potak proclaimed.

Potak held the glass ball like it was dangerous and he quickly passed it back to the small boy. It immediately came alive in dazzling brilliance. All four of them had to shade their eyes with their hands. Delbert slipped it back into its pouch as it became clear to

Potak, the ball was somehow intertwined with the young boys and the cosmos.

"I see its magic belongs only to you and your friend," Potak said in wonderment. "If you ask it a question for me, will it give you an answer?"

"I don't know," Del replied.

"Try it," Potak said with a smile. "Ask it where my cousin and I are to go this spring. I know a journey lies ahead, but we still don't know where it will take us. Maybe you can help us find our destiny. In return, perhaps we can help you find what you seek."

Del again slipped the perfect sphere from its leather sheath and, as soon as he wrapped his small hands around it, a golden light seemed to appear deep at the center of the ball. As the light intensified, Dell opened his hands and the crystal began to spin between his palms, a swirling mass of light and energy.

This time, Potak's eyes widened as the sphere made shadows dance across the walls of the cavern.

The ball had no effect on the small teen, who looked down at the spinning globe and asked, "Where will our two new friends go? What is their path for the New Year?" Del asked.

He tilted his head to one side as if someone was whispering in his ear and he nodded his head. His hands trembled as if he was again freezing. The crystal was reacting with his body. When the trembling stopped, Potak felt sure an answer was forthcoming.

"It says your new path is one with ours," Del said. When he said it, his voice seemed to come from some distant place, deeper and more masculine.

Potak was sure the crystal had provided them with an omen or a vision. He wondered how it was possible

for young boys, with no obvious knowledge of the spirits, to possess such an object. Even though Potak had
the answer to his question, now he was more perplexed
than ever. Somehow the two strange young men were
intertwined in their destiny.

How could that be, and what lay ahead?

8. ANOTHER STORM

In a secluded cave in Seminole Canyon, Texas

"IF WE ARE TO TRAVEL THE SAME PATH, TELL US WHAT IT IS you seek," Potak asked.

"Esmeralda and Liberty said if we traveled to Texas, we would find the parents we have not seen in many years," Tommy said. "They have been lost to us."

"What do you mean, lost?" Tuc asked.

"My father abandoned me shortly after my birth," Delbert explained. "I have no memory of him."

"And my mother disappeared before my tenth birthday," Tommy added. "She was stolen against her will and has not been heard from since."

Tuc looked at his cousin. He shook his head and said, "I do not understand White people."

"Perhaps we should not judge these people until we find them and ask them why they have not tried to reunite with their sons," Potak said.

"Do you mean you are going to help us?" Tommy asked.

"It appears our destinies are intertwined for that purpose," Potak replied.

As usual, Tuc was angered by his cousin's reply. He hated it when the spirits led him and his cousin on long, endless treks across Texas. He shook his head and frowned.

Feeling one with the spirit world, Potak smiled and noticed the boys could barely keep their eyes open. The heat of the cave had enveloped them. With their bellies full, their once cold and trembling muscles sought rest.

"You have traveled far," he said. "I can see the weariness in your young eyes. Let us sleep and we will speak of our future in the morning."

The warmth of the fire was so comforting, Tommy leaned against the wall and allowed his long legs to stretch across the width of the cave. He draped an arm around Delbert, who leaned into the warmth of his friend's girth, and quickly was overcome by sleep. The leather pouch that held the crystal ball slipped from the small one's hand and rested in the lap of the giant.

"Greenhorns!" Tuc grunted. "These are two of the oddest White people I have ever met. I am not so sure they don't use magic to deceive us. "

"I don't know," Potak said. "You know I am drawn to magic. I want to learn more. I feel our destinies have been joined for a reason."

"I hope you aren't wrong. We can sleep on it," Tuc said.

Disgusted, he placed his bedroll next to the fire and retired for the night. He hoped Potak would rethink his decision by the time morning arrived. In the back of his mind, he knew his cousin seldom did what he wished. It was always about visions and messages from the spirit world.

Sleep was far from Potak's mind. Too many questions plagued his thoughts. He wished the Wandering Tree was there to help him envision what was to come. Instead, he again stuffed his pipe with the herbal mixture and lit it with a burning ember.

Outside, the winter storm whistled and howled, coating every living thing in ice and snow. The temperature dropped, and snow drifted across the entrance of the cave.

Potak inhaled and exhaled copious amounts of smoke as it swirled around his head. He reached for the leather pouch as his ally—smoke—opened his mind to the spirit world. His heart rate slowed as the magic of the potion pulsed through his veins. He let the crystal ball slip from the leather pouch, and he gripped it in one hand, closed his eyes, and waited to see if something would happen. After some time, a vision appeared. Potak's heart began to race and now thundered between his ears.

He felt his body being pulled upward and away from the cave in a white whirlwind of snow and ice. It roared with amazing energy he had never before experienced. Ice and snow stung his cheeks and brow as the torrent spun and carried him high into the clouds. The next thing he knew, the sun was peaking over the horizon and its warmth replaced the cold. He had risen above the clouds and storm.

A blue haze blocked his view of where he had been transported. He used his arms to make an opening in the apparent fog. His hands parted the cloud like a curtain. It opened a window in time from which the old shaman could observe people from some other dimension—some other place.

As he peered down through the opening, a woman with long blonde hair appeared before the shaman's eyes. She was tall and curvaceous. The folds of her dress ruffled lightly as she walked. She was serving drinks to several men in an elaborate parlor.

Potak heard a soft female voice call to her and say, "Em, Room 16 needs a bottle of our finest whiskey. Take it to them immediately." A trace of perfume wafted in the air for just a moment, just long enough for Potak to inhale it. His senses came alive and he grew more curious.

When she turned to retrieve the bottle of spirits, Potak could not believe his eyes. The White woman had a full beard that was as yellow as the hair that hung down to her shoulders and across her back. Her blonde beard fell in waves across her breasts.

The medicine man had never seen a woman—red, white, or black—with a beard. What did it mean? He rubbed his eyes with his knuckles. Maybe he was imagining things. But such was the way of the spirit world— to seek revelation.

Could this be one of the people the boys are searching for?

When he looked down a second time, the parlor scene became difficult to see. It began to fall away like grains of sand. Small clouds of particles replaced the first vision with a second. As the last molecules of the first image were swept away by an invisible wind, a second seemed to form before his very eyes. As the image was reconstructed, he now saw a White man's courtroom. A spindly old man in a black robe with hair growing out his ears banged his wooden hammer on his bench and shouted, "Jack Elliott, you have been found guilty by a jury of your peers. You have been found guilty on all counts and will be held in the county jail until which time you can be transported to the state penitentiary. There, you will serve a sentence of five years of hard labor."

"But Your Honor, I'm innocent," the accused pleaded. "I didn't do any of those things. I was nowhere near the livery when it happened."

"A jury of your peers has decided otherwise, Mr. Elliott. Take him away!" the judge ordered as his eyes blazed and he pulled on the whiskers of his chin.

The man shouted his innocence as he was ushered away. The eyes of those in the courtroom showed scorn.

Suddenly the vision disappeared as mysteriously as it appeared. It was replaced with a clear blue sky. Immediately, the spiraling mass of the storm returned below him. As the stillness of the storm's eye collapsed, Potak squeezed the leather pouch and crystal ball tightly so it wouldn't slip away. He closed his eyes as he was drawn down into the tornado-like spiral of particles. Tiny pieces of ice peppered his skin and extreme cold made his joints ache. He could hear nothing above the roar of the torrent.

* * *

POTAK LAY on the warm cave floor in a deep, deep sleep as his feet and hands twitched. His pupils fluttered under his eyelids like he was attempting to awaken but could not break away from his deep slumber. Tuc nudged his shoulder with the toe of his moccasin, and his cousin mumbled something indecipherable. The Tonkawa warrior nudged him again and the shaman blinked twice and then peered up and into his cousin's eyes.

"Why did you interfere with my dream? You know I don't like to be awakened. What if you had disturbed an important vision?" he grumbled as he rubbed the sleep from his eyes with the palms of his hands.

"The storm has passed, and I had to make our morning coffee. It's still hot. It's time for you to get up. It's unlike you to sleep beyond sunrise. Are you sick or just getting old?" his cousin asked. He was grumpy as usual, but the angry voice did not match the concern in his eyes.

"Of course, I'm not sick and you are just as old as me. I'm fine. Since when do I need to seek your approval to sleep? I can sleep or awaken whenever I wish," Potak bristled.

"The boys have gone out to check on their animals. Without shelter, I doubt anything could have survived last night's storm. They should be back soon. What are we going to do with this odd pair?"

"Why did you let them go out alone?" Potak asked scoldingly. "You can see they are out of their depths in the wilderness. They might get lost and we will have to find them."

"You were the one who invited them to our cave and gave them food," Tuc retorted. "Nobody made me their babysitter. What do you plan to do with these strange and green fools? I say we leave them somewhere safe, and we continue on our journey."

"We will let the spirits guide us, as always," Potak said. He smiled knowingly and added, "We cannot abandon them now that we have taken them in and given them food. I feel they are part of our next journey. You know we cannot change our destiny. I had a vision."

"You're always having visions, and what about the mysterious ball? I have a bad feeling about this object. You heard them. The magic ball belonged to a witch! Female witches are the most dangerous kind."

Potak smiled as he held the leather pouch, which felt heavy in his grasp. The magic crystal was inside. It swung like a pendulum from two fingers. Tuc's jaw muscles tightened as his eyes moved back and forth following the movement of the strange object. The cousins often didn't need to talk to communicate. It was almost like they were telepathic, and the medicine man knew when his cousin felt fear. It was an emotion Tuc seldom experienced.

"What are you doing with that?" Tuc asked, showing surprise despite his warrior's face. He took two steps back as if it was poison.

"It assisted me on a vision last night," the medicine man replied with a smile.

"Was it enlightening? Did you see the future?"

"Yes," the shaman said with some deep peacefulness in his eyes. Something had changed. "It has a special magic."

Tuc shook his head and said, "You don't have to say anymore. I know you've already made up your mind without asking me. We are going to help these odd characters find their parents, aren't we? You are getting soft in your old age, cousin."

"Do not worry. It is the time of the solstice. There will be little danger where we are going," Potak said as his smile grew.

"Your eyes tell a different story, cousin."

"I had a vision. Actually, I had two, which is very uncommon. I have seen the loved ones the strange young men seek out. No wonder they are so odd. The woman they are looking for has a beard."

Tuc huffed as if his cousin was playing with him for doubting his visions. He knew women did not have beards, just as men did not have antlers.

"You don't believe me, do you?" Potak asked as he chuckled. "I don't blame you. Had I not seen the vision with my own eyes I wouldn't have believed it either."

Once Tuc realized his cousin was serious, he was even more concerned. He felt danger lay in wait for them.

"If she has a beard, it is proof she is a witch," Tuc whispered as if the spirits were listening.

Potak belly-laughed, something he had not done for a long time. It felt good. This journey seemed like something different—something special. He felt it was not as dangerous as his cousin thought it might be. He felt it was a time to give and share. In return, he would be allowed the possibility to learn from the magic ball.

"What did the boys say when they discovered the ball was missing?" Potak asked. "Were they angry?"

"The large boy became scared at first. It was in his lap. His small friend was who saw it in your grasp. So, he let it be. I don't think they understand the full power of the crystal ball any more than I do. They left just as puzzled as me."

Potak threw his blanket off and unfolded his thin frame. He stood and stretched. His face wrinkled before the fire like an old dog. He stretched his arms above his head as though he had awoken from a weeklong sleep. His joints no longer hurt, and his arthritis seemed to have disappeared. There was a twinkle in his eyes.

9. OFF TO BIG SPRING, TEXAS

POTAK FELT THE WEIGHT OF THE LEATHER POUCH IN HIS hand. Sometimes it seemed as light as a feather and other times it weighed as heavy as a brick. It seemed to have a life of its own. He wondered where it would take them next. But first, they had to see if the greenhorns could find their way back to the cave.

Potak believed it was not the boys who had found them; it was the crystal ball that sought out the cousins. The boys were just part of the journey as was he and Tuc. The exact location where it would lead them was still unknown. The prospect of this new journey felt different, though. Danger always lurks in the wilderness, so he knew any journey was susceptible to the evil deeds of men. The essence of the coming path carried a new and fresh meaning, unlike many of the violent journeys of the past.

Potak also knew the spirits were crafty and liked to play jokes on mere mortals, and he could never wholly trust them. So, although he had nothing but good feelings about their future, he did not disregard Tuc's caution and reluctance. His cousin had unique powers that enhanced his warrior skills. They were powers Potak didn't possess.

As always, they would need to tread lightly as they sought out the bearded lady and the man who was sent to jail. He wondered if the two strange boys would be welcomed by their parents or be shunned. They had abandoned both boys in the past.

As usual, there were far more questions than there were answers. Fortunately, Potak felt the path they were to follow promised joy and good tidings, but he was unsure why.

When the Tonkawa Indians heard the boys struggling to climb the slippery path to the cave, both were surprised they had found their way back on their own. Maybe the pair were more resourceful than they had originally thought. The large one was very strong and would be a difficult opponent for an Indian and the small one appeared to have knowledge beyond his years. He had all the features of a normal human but was abnormally small. Now, only time would tell if they would be happy with the destiny chosen for them.

The minute the odd pair stepped back into the cave, Potak felt the crystal warm within the pouch he held in his palm. Similarly, he understood the message of his two visions. He knew where to go to find the boys' missing family members. It came as a whisper he heard clearly without having to raise the crystal ball to his ear. He listened intently to a voice that seemed far away.

"They found their way safely back," Tuc whispered as he cocked his head to listen and grumbled as if he was disappointed. "We aren't really going to lead these two, are we?"

"The power of the magic ball is drawing me toward their path," Potak said with half-closed eyes. He acted as if he had one foot in the present and the other in the world of the spirits. "This journey will carry us to the coming summer, but there are secrets hidden within the path we must travel. They will be revealed as we travel with these odd boys at our side. We must not ignore the vision. It could be dangerous if we don't heed the messages and warnings."

"Are you going to agree to take them to find their family?" Tuc asked, now clearly angry. "You have always said it could be dangerous not to follow your vision. I believe you say this to trick me into going."

Tuc looked deep into his cousin's eyes and said, "You don't have to go if you don't want to. I have never forced you to follow me, brother."

Potak knew his cousin felt responsible for his safety and would never allow him to venture into an unknown situation if it would put his life in danger. The few times Tuc let Potak wander off on his own, he eventually had to go find him. He knew he could not say no. That did not mean he was going to go happily. No, not Tuc.

"You know I'll go but don't expect me to babysit these two if they begin to cry," Tuc huffed. "There is nothing I hate worse than greenhorns and white boys."

When Tommy and Del clawed their way to the top, Tuc chuckled. They were both shivering again, although the snow had stopped. The sun was now blazing, making the glare impossible to look at. It was a bright new day, and the temperature began to rise nearly as fast as it had fallen two days before.

Potak knew they first would head for Big Spring. He had only been there once, but he had often been to

Signal Peak, sixteen miles to the south. It was a place the native tribes used to send smoke signals long distances. Because of its towering height, the messages could be seen for many miles in every direction. It was also a place where Potak had gone to seek spiritual guidance. He often sought out high places because they were closer to the spirit world.

Big Springs had long been a popular watering hole for many Native American Indians and nomads, mostly Jumano, Apache, and Comanche. The Comanche had used the watering hole to assemble and organize their large-scale war parties. Their raids into northern Mexico were many during the Comanche-Mexican Wars. It also was an entry point for the Overland Trail to California.

The settlement sprung up around 1870 and was populated mainly by buffalo hunters who frequented the area. As soon as the Texas & Pacific Railroad built a station there in the 1880s, it became a town. Much like Abilene and Colorado City—similar communities that catered to the railroad and ranchers—saloons and gambling dens flourished in Big Spring. Where there was money, there always was crime. Where there was a crime, the White men had now brought the law. The law could not exist without courts and courthouses.

It was in a courtroom Potak envisioned the small boy's father. Fortunately, it was not far. Even in bad weather, they could get there safely.

* * *

ALTHOUGH THE BOYS were near frozen from the trek back from the bottom of the mountain, Delbert immediately noticed Potak was holding the pouch and crystal ball. He released a loud burst of air and his trembling slowed.

"Thank goodness you have the crystal, Potak," the small teen said. "I was scared to death we had lost it in the snow. That is why we took so long to return. We searched everywhere."

"My feet are frozen from kicking snowbanks," Tommy said and shivered.

"You didn't look everywhere," Tuc scoffed, "because it was right here."

"It was in Tommy's lap when you fell asleep last night," Potak explained and handed it back to the tall one. "I retrieved it for safekeeping. I did not want it to roll away."

Potak held the pouch by the strings and handed it to the tall boy. Tommy's frozen body stopped shaking the second he touched the orb. He kneeled and placed it between his ear and Delbert's.

A huge smile spread across the small boy's face and he asked, "Do you have good news for us?"

"Perhaps you had a vision," Tommy queried.

"The crystal says both of you possess great spiritual powers, and you will join our quest to find our parents. Is this true?" Del asked joyfully.

"I don't like this person whose voice speaks from the glass ball," Tuc said and scowled.

The teens looked at the fierce warrior with skepticism. They did not know how he could dislike someone he had never encountered.

"You would like her if you knew her," Tommy said. "She cured my body. I used to be slow and clumsy; now I am strong and can do many things easily."

"Yet you could not find your way out of the storm," Tuc replied condescendingly.

"You are older and smarter than we are," Delbert said, sticking up for his best friend. "Have you considered the fact that perhaps the crystal guided us here so you would find us and offer your help?"

"I believe in the spirit world, not a piece of glass," Tuc said and walked toward the fire.

"Your friend, David Hart, would not doubt the crystal," Tommy said as he tucked the leather pouch in his pocket.

Tuc stopped and turned abruptly. "What do you know of Lieutenant Davie?" Tuc asked with a look of surprise on his face. His knuckles turned white as his fingers gripped his knife.

"We know nothing of him. Esmeralda says he was a White man you trusted," Tommy replied.

"You can trust us, too," Delbert said.

"We will see!" Tuc snorted and walked to the fire.

"Don't mind Tuc," Potak explained. "He trusts no one and tends to be grumpy in the morning."

"What you call grumpy, I call protective, cousin," Tuc said sourly. "Have I ever failed to keep you safe, wherever your crazy treks have led?"

"You have never failed, and I appreciate it," Potak said.

Potak turned his attention to the boys and stated, "The good news is we begin our search for your parents in Big Spring, which is not far from here."

The boys' eyes lit up.

"When do we start?" Del asked.

"We will eat first," Potak said. "I have not yet had my coffee."

"If you wouldn't have slept..." Tuc snarled but was stopped at mid-sentence when his cousin held up his hand.

"Don't forget, sleep sometimes is the link that unites us with the spirits. Without sleep, we might wander aimlessly."

"Hrumph!" was the only sound that came from his sour cousin.

"The answer to your question, little man, is yes. We will help you on your quest. The winter solstice approaches, and we must do good. Come and warm yourselves by the fire before we begin our journey," Potak said.

When they all settled around the fire, Tuc asked, "I must ask if you found your animals and are they in need of care?"

"No, they either ran off or succumbed to the freezing temperatures," Del said.

"I don't like the snow," Tommy said. "Ichabod always took the touring company south for the winter. So, we've never experienced weather like this."

"Nor have we. Texas can get cold, but never this cold," Tuc said.

"The sun is strong now and will warm us on our journey. As soon as we finish eating, it will be time to begin," the medicine man said.

* * *

WHEN THE ODD foursome arrived in Big Spring, the temperature had risen to minus five degrees. As it was still below freezing, the four travelers knew they would have to find shelter for the night before they began to search for Delbert's father. According to Potak's vision, he was in jail. The ground was still covered with snow, so they made their way to the livery stables, the only place an Indian could pay to spend the night. Potak remembered it from his first visit to this settlement, which consisted mainly of rawhide huts, saloons, and brothels.

The temperature began to drop as the sun neared the horizon, and a crisp blue sky lay overhead. The snowstorm had passed, but it was still too cold for inexperienced boys to sleep on the frozen ground. The setting sun was no more than a prism of color in a white haze.

The man in charge of the Big Springs stables was only a head taller than Del and had curly red hair. His legs were bowed from a life on horseback. He waddled when he walked. His cheek bulged with a wad of tobacco, and he held a tin can he used as a spittoon. Brown juice dripped from the edge of his mouth.

"That'll be two bits for the four of ya per night, gents," the stableman said and grinned. "They call me Red. You boys can sleep in the hayloft where it's a mite warmer. There's a cast-iron stove over there in the corner. If you want to warm your hands and make a coffee. My room is right behind that door, so don't ya try to sneak off with any of my horses. I'm a light sleeper. I'm an early riser, too. So, I'm gonna turn in now. Sweet dreams, boys."

In minutes Potak had a pot of coffee brewing as the pungent aroma of boiling java mixed with the smell of horse manure and hay. Tuc pulled his large knife from its sheath. Both boys gasped. Their eyes bugged wide with fright; they had never seen such a big knife. Tuc smiled, which made him look fiercer. Then he split up a dozen pieces of wood and used his knife to flip the metal lever to open the pot-bellied stove. He stoked it with wood making heat radiate through the room. The waves of warmth were almost visible. Potak tossed some salted pork and beans in a second pot and began to prepare a meal for the four of them.

"Do you think my pa is in jail here?" Del asked.

"If he is the man in my vision, yes," Potak replied. "Or maybe the man in jail will provide the path to your father. Visions and spirits are tricky. Often, they appear to mean one thing and turn into something else. We will have to go to the sheriff's office tomorrow to see."

"I don't like going to the White man's jails," Tuc retorted. "What if they decide to lock us up or hang us?"

"Tommy and Del can go ask the sheriff if the man in the lockup is Jack Elliott. There is nothing illegal about such a request. We run no risk. We can wait outside in case they have some unforeseen problem."

"You trust White people too much, cousin," Tuc spat.

"What does it hurt to be kind to someone, whether they be red like us or white like the boys? What does skin color have to do with anything, for that matter? When we die, we are all the same as when we are born. Our blood is of the same color, too."

The next morning, a cold wind blew as they made their way from the stables to the building in the middle of the small town. They leaned into the wind as they walked. The four travelers made deep footprints in the fresh snow. Down the street, there was a gray sign with black letters swinging in the wind. It said: Sheriff's Office and US Post Office. As they approached, they could see the windows at the rear of the building down the alley were covered with bars. Yellow light showed in the front windows from oil lamps with wicks turned up. Despite the hour, the daylight was dull from the winter haze.

Potak wrapped his bearskin high around his neck to ward off the winter wind. He could see the two boys tremble in the freezing air. It felt like ice against their faces. They wore woolen coats, but they did not protect them from the elements like the animal furs the Indians used.

Before they got too near the jail, Tuc removed his revolver from his belt and hid it in his bag. An armed Indian is always a target in a White man's town. It was good to have it handy, but he didn't want anyone to get the wrong idea about their intentions. Tommy towered over the three, and Del didn't reach Tuc's chest. They made for strange companions in any man's town.

Tuc leaned his back against the leeward side of the building, as did Potak, to stay out of the wind. He cupped his hands near his mouth and blew into them to warm them. Snowdrifts stood deep on the windward side of the wooden buildings along the street. Not a living soul could be seen. It was still early, and most folks had not gotten up the determination to weather the chill.

"Go ahead and ask," Tuc grumbled. "I don't want to stand out here all day."

Potak smiled and nodded his head understandingly. His kind eyes gave the boys confidence.

"Go on, children," Potak ordered as he lay his hands on their shoulders. "Go find your destiny."

The boys' big eyes blinked innocently like babies.

They knew they stood on the door of discovery. The answers to one of their lifelong questions were close at hand. They were about to venture into a new world and a new journey. They had no idea if it would be joyful or sad.

10. JACK ELLIOTT

Somewhere in western Louisiana

JACK ELLIOTT HAD NEVER BEEN A LUCKY MAN. IT SEEMED like everything he touched turned to shit. It wasn't that he didn't try or wasn't a hard worker. When there was a job to do, he always toiled twice as hard as the rest of the men. He often worked from dawn to dusk seven days a week without a complaint. Unfortunately, bad luck was his constant companion. It perched on his shoulder and pecked at him like a hungry vulture. Everything he did, no matter how noble or how significant, always turned upside down. He felt he had been cursed from the day he was born.

Jack stretched five inches beyond six feet and stood out in a crowd because of his size, which suited him for an array of jobs Ichabod Justice needed him to perform in support of the touring company. Elliott enjoyed the variety and was a valuable asset.

The entourage was in its winter home when his first and only son was born, making Jack the happiest man in the world. When his wife, Estar, passed just days after the child was born, his life imploded.

The loss of his wife was devastating, but Jack tried to spend all his free time doting on the baby with the aid of an old Black nanny, named Matty, who lived nearby. Being the caravan of Marvels was idle for several months, Jack sought part-time work. He failed at every job he landed, though. No matter how hard he tried, he fouled things up.

When he landed a job at the general store in town, he thought he was providing stability for little Delbert. The child was small but looked exactly like his mother. Every time Jack looked at him, he was reminded of his beloved Estar, tiny and lovable.

All was going well. Jack's luck finally had changed, he thought, and he was enjoying fatherhood with the help of Matty. His employer considered him the perfect employee. He was tall enough to reach the top shelves in the store of the haberdashery without a ladder. He was so strong he could lift heavy barrels and boxes with such ease the owner no longer had to struggle with moving the supplies from one place to another. Store-owner Harold Belching suffered from a bad back, and Elliot's presence meant he could leave the heavy work to his employee. At first, it seemed Jack was a gift from God. As usual, though, Jack's constant companion, bad luck, caught up with him.

Once a week, Elliot hitched up Belching's old gray mare to the store's buckboard wagon and delivered special supplies to neighboring ranches. His deliveries generally went to a half dozen of his boss's best clients.

His fortunes changed on a cool autumn day when tragedy struck. His wagon was loaded with giant spools of barbed wire for the cattle ranches and heavy blocks of salt for the livestock. He also had supplies for a nearby farmer, who had ordered seeds for bell peppers, broccoli, cabbage, and a variety of farm utilities.

Jack was less than five miles out of town when he ran across an old fellow with a broken wheel on his carriage. He had seen the same man around town on occasion, so he felt no danger. Whenever Elliot saw a neighbor in trouble, he didn't hesitate to stop and assist.

The man had repaired the wheel strap and was struggling to use a long tree branch as leverage to lift the wagon high enough to replace the wheel. He couldn't do it single-handed. So, Elliot stepped down from his wagon to assist. With his strength, he quickly lifted the carriage so the man could slip the wheel back onto the axle.

That was when he got the surprise of his life. Two more men burst from the bushes with pistols aimed his way.

"Don't make a move there, big fella," a man dressed in a buckskin shirt, denim pants, and knee-high boots growled. He cocked his pistol and pointed the barrel at Elliot. Both robbers wore burlap hoods over their faces to hide their identities.

"Make one move, and I'll blow you away, big boy," the outlaw said.

The old gentleman he had helped turned on Elliot with an evil grin and said, "See whatcha get for being the good Samaritan, you big fool? Now, you've gone and lost your cargo, your wagon, and a team of horses to boot."

The older man snickered and spat into the dirt at the large man's feet. Before he turned to leave in his repaired carriage, he nodded and winked at the two bandits.

Elliot just stood in disbelief as the old man sped off toward town. The two highwaymen climbed onto the seat of the buckboard wagon, filled with supplies, and drove off in the opposite direction. Elliot could not believe he allowed himself to be snookered and robbed without a bullet shot or even a tussle. He knew his goose was cooked. His boss was going to be furious, and nobody would believe he was tricked out of the supplies, which were of considerable value. Of course, Elliot didn't have the money to pay his employer for the loss.

Jack didn't know what to do. So, he turned for the town and walked back to the general store. What would he tell his boss? More importantly, would the store owner believe he had been robbed?

It took him nearly two hours to walk back to town. All the way back he ran what happened over and over in his mind, so he had his story straight for when he arrived and fessed up. As soon as he was near enough to see the general store, he spotted the man with the broken-down carriage, the same individual who had initiated the theft.

The carriage owner and Belching were talking on the porch. The old man was making wild gestures with his hands as Jack approached. When they got sight of Elliot, the man who helped rob him began to jump up and down and point his finger his way.

"That there's the fella I saw selling your goods to some bandits just outside of town!" the carriage owner yelled.

From the corner of his eye, Elliot saw the town

sheriff coming toward him. The lawman had his hand on his revolver, and his eyes shot daggers at the accused thief. Of course, the big brute's face showed nothing but shock. He couldn't understand what was going on. He gathered all the courage he could muster and walked the final steps to the store, where the men awaited him.

"That's him!" the carriage owner claimed as he stomped his foot and pointed his finger at Elliot. "He was in cahoots with those thieves. I seen him do it."

Of course, he was innocent of any crime, but no matter how many times he told the sheriff his story, the lies of the respected town citizen carried more weight. Not a trace was found of the stolen supplies, and Elliot was unceremoniously thrown into jail.

To make things worse, not two hours after his arrest, the jail wagon pulled up before the sheriff's office to transport prisoners to a nearby town with a courthouse and judge. Jack was the victim of a vile ruse and being railroaded with little or no defense.

Everything happened so quickly. Jack didn't even have time to get word to Matty, who was caring for his son.

Before he knew it, he was loaded into the back of a wagon with an iron bar cage attached to the bed. Inside were five more criminals. Elliot was the only honest man among them, but that mattered little to the deputy marshal who drove the team. He knew all convicts claimed to be innocent but were guilty as sin. They all deserved to be locked up.

Elliott was judged and convicted without legal representation. He was sentenced to five years behind bars. The same lawman who arrested him initially carried him off to the penitentiary where he would serve his time. The wagon's wheels squeaked and kicked up dust as a tear rolled down Elliott's cheek. His life had taken another turn and he was leaving his son and civilization behind.

The prison where Jack was held was like lockups everywhere. It was more like a school for professional criminals than a conduit for reformation. Most of Elliot's cellmates were hardened crooks and thieves, who exchanged their trade secrets with the prison community. An innocent man could easily learn to be a crook.

Lucky for Elliot, he was big and strong. Other convicts didn't harass or bully him as they did in town. He no longer was the big galoot others ridiculed and taunted for being as dumb as an ox. In prison, power and strength meant men respected you. It wasn't long until one of the heads of the prison gangs took him under his wing.

"Dirty" Dave Kinter was one of the prison's power brokers, despite being sentenced to a life term for murder. He had his fingers into every illegal activity in the lockup. His most prized scheme was the making of "prison hooch" and selling it for absurd prices.

In the pen, men would do anything for Kinter's poison brew. It helped them tolerate the prison's filth and abuse. In six months, Jack became Kinter's official bodyguard. He no longer was a big oaf; he was a man of importance.

Elliot's mind soon was poisoned by his surroundings. He saw how flawed the justice system was. He figured if they accused him of being an outlaw, he might as well reap the rewards.

As Kinter's enforcer, life behind bars became a little

easier. If someone needed to be taught a lesson, Jack was the teacher. If an arm or leg had to be broken to make a point, Jack was big enough to snap most bones with his bare hands. Even the prison guards gave way to the mountain of a man. He and Kinter ruled within the stone walls and nobody dared cross them.

Along with the freedom to do whatever he wanted in the penitentiary, Kinter paid him with any contraband he wanted and all the "hooch" he could consume.

Jack had never been one to consume alcohol, but he quickly became addicted to Kinter's brew. Before he knew it, he needed it to sleep at night and to feel better in the morning. He had a shot at lunchtime and always before he had to enforce Kinter's will on some poor inmate.

He became as vile as Kinter himself.

After four years and ten months behind bars, to Jack's great surprise, he was released. He figured it was part of Kinter's doing and the new warden wanting to rid the prison corridors of the brutal enforcer.

When he was released, Jack found a spot as far away from people as he could find. He camped in the wilderness and scavenged for food. He tangled with the withdrawal from Kinter's "hooch" and a lifestyle he knew was unacceptable. It took two weeks before his mind and body were ready to face civilization. When he stepped away from his meager campsite, he promised his late wife he would never stoop so low as to allow himself to be imprisoned again.

11. REGRETTABLE PAST

Somewhere near the Texas border

WITH HIS SELF-HEALING COMPLETED, THE FIRST THING Jack did was return to Bawcomville, Louisiana, the winter home of the Justice Touring Company. He hoped to reunite with his son. Since his incarceration, the once small community had grown and changed dramatically; nothing was the same.

Belching's General Store was gone, as was the hostel and the nanny with whom Elliott had entrusted his son's care. Where could they have gone? The sheriff and all previous acquaintances shunned him. No one was willing to provide any kind of aid to a convicted thief. The sheriff threatened to arrest him again if he didn't leave town immediately.

Jack was lost and distraught.

He wandered from town to town and reneged on his promise to Estar. He saw the inside of more jails than he could count. Each time he was released, he started anew. He devoted his days and nights to finding Delbert. His mind was overwhelmed with thoughts of his son. Had he survived childhood? Where was he? Who was taking care of him? What was he like?

Jack prayed he was nothing like his old man, big and stupid. He once was an honorable, hard-working man with a wife and family. Now, he was impoverished, no more than a vagrant and a convict.

Unbeknownst to Jack, Matty had returned his son to the Marvelous Marvels Touring Company when it returned to its winter home. There was no opportunity for a Black woman to raise a White child on her own in the South; life was hard enough without such a burden. The Elliott baby would make her an outcast in both communities, White and Black, and she could ill afford another mouth to feed.

The situation was compounded by the fact the child was the smallest baby she had ever laid eyes upon. He just didn't grow like other children. Clearly, he had inherited his mother's genes and would be a dwarf and require doctoring. So, it seemed right to return the child to his origins, Ichabod Justice's troupe of misfits and odd characters.

The caravan always returned home with a certain amount of hoopla. As usual, they came back on a December afternoon and made camp along the Ouachita River. With tiny Delbert wrapped in a blanket and cradled in her arms, Matty knocked at the trailer door of Ichabod Justice on December 23rd, two days before Christmas.

"I'm sorry to disturb you, Mr. Justice. I is Matty Fairweather and this here be Delbert Elliott. He da son of

Estar and Jack Elliott, who done got himself arrested and thrown in prison."

"Come in! Come in!" Justice said with a warm smile. "I recall Jack and Estar fondly. She was one of our star performers, bless her soul. Did you say this is her son?"

"Yessum! Mr. Elliott pays me to care for da child afore he gets himself in trouble. Now, he is gone and Matty can't care no more for his child. You take him. He be more suited for your kind than mine," the nanny demanded.

She pushed the child into Ichabod's arms and ran off without another word. Justice was shocked by the sudden turn of events. He had no idea what to do next. His heart melted, though, when he looked at the cooing child. With his dark hair and brown eyes, he was a spitting image of his mother.

Estar Elliott made the troupe a lot of money before her sudden and untimely death. Maybe this child could, too, he surmised. So, he marched directly to the trailer of Henrietta Hutchins, whose heart was as big as she was.

"I have an early Christmas present for you," Ichabod told the large woman as he placed the bundle in her arms.

"What is this?" she asked.

"It is the child of Estar Elliott," the entrepreneur said. "It seems Jack has run off and the child has been abandoned. I know you and Estar were friends, and I thought you would not mind caring for the babe until we can find out what happened to Jack. I'll gladly pay you a monthly stipend for his care."

"Of course, Ichabod," she replied, beaming at the small child. "My word, he looks just like his mother."

"I know you will need diapers and milk," he said. "I'll run into town and secure whatever you need. I might even come back with a cow. Reckon it might be nice to have milk regularly."

Miss Hutchins nodded her approval. In the surrogate mother's eyes, the child was more marvelous than any of the characters who worked for Ichabod Justice, and Delbert got the loving home he deserved. Christmas was going to be grand for Miss Hutchins, and she didn't care if Jack Elliott ever was found.

* * *

PENNILESS AND WITH his son gone, Jack quickly relied on the only trade he knew, outlawing. It was not the life he would have chosen but the one forced on him. His old friend, BAD LUCK, continued to ride his shoulder, just as a raven accompanies the grim reaper as he steals human souls. His life had turned from a bright and happy one to that of sadness and dread. Marked as an outlaw and convict, he believed there was no going back. As they say in prison, "Once an outlaw, always an outlaw."

When he was released from a two-month stint behind bars, prison officials claimed they had lost the few belongings and clothing he had with him when he was apprehended. So, he was provided standard issue bib overalls that marked him as a recent prisoner.

Jack knew he had to get rid of his clothing as quickly as possible or be recognized like every other convict released from the state prison. So, he began to walk in the direction of the nearest town and hoped to find what he needed along the way.

He learned in prison it always was preferable to commit a crime as far away from civilization as possible so any response would be slow. Certainly, the opportunity to form a posse and give chase was lessened.

After several hours of walking, he came to the far outskirts of Brownsville. Beside a greenhouse, a variety of clothing festooned on a clothesline. There were bright-colored shirts and blue pants, red long johns, women's skirts, and knickers. The breeze ruffled Jack's black hair and he pushed it out of his face. As he eyed the clothing, it was apparent it belonged to a family with several members.

Jack was a difficult man to fit due to his size, but luck would have it there was a large man in the household. He carefully made his way around the country home and to the stables in the back, always making sure he was out of sight. He immediately spotted a half dozen horses, saddles, and tack. He climbed into the second story of the small stable and burrowed into a pile of hay so he could hide until nightfall.

He could tell it was nearing dark as the light that came through the stable doors was diminishing. He felt his time was near. He began to push the hay aside so he could get a better look if anyone was outside. That was when he heard someone making their way up the wooden ladder that led to the haystack. Jack froze. He didn't want to be detected, but he still wanted to peek at the man through the layers of hay that covered him. His heart nearly stopped when the man grabbed the pitchfork and began to toss hay to the ground floor to feed the livestock.

The first stab of the rusty forks went right between his legs. He wished he had a weapon. The man was nearly as large as him, and, without a knife or gun, defending himself would be difficult. With each stab of the pointed barbs, Jack was sure he would be wounded or worse. The pile quickly was diminishing. He feared his discovery was imminent. With the last stab of the pitchfork, one of the tines punctured his buttocks. He had to bite his lip to keep from screaming. Jack was more angry than hurt. Rivulets of blood ran from his bit lip down his chin. Fortunately, he remained out of sight.

Finally, the homeowner propped the pitchfork back up against the support beam and scrambled back down the wooden ladder and began to brush down the horses. Things were becoming more complicated than Jack had expected. Bad luck continued to nag at him and bite at his heels with every turn and every decision he made.

It was well over an hour before the man closed the stable's double doors and disappeared. It was pitch black. Finally, Jack had a small bit of luck. He peeked through a tiny loft door and noticed the women of the house had not taken in the washing. So, Jack shimmied down the ladder as quickly as he could and ran for the clothesline. He pulled down what he needed and then scrambled back to the hayloft to wait for the house lights to go out. He quickly changed his clothing and tore a piece from his old shirt to make a bandage for his punctured buttocks. The ex-con lay hidden for so long, he eventually fell asleep.

He awoke with a start, guessing he had slept the night, and with the dawn of the next day, his capture was inevitable. His breath became short and blood thundered between his ears. The last thing he wanted was to be discovered.

He was in luck, though. It was still dark and all was quiet. He saddled the best horse he could find as quietly as he could and walked the horse across the fields behind the back of the house. When he was far enough away, he mounted up and kicked the horse's flanks. He leaned into the horse as if he was in a race for his life. For Jack, it was.

He had not only stolen some clothing but a horse and saddle as well. Horse thievery was a hanging offense in most states. He noted this was the first real crime he had ever committed, despite spending five years in prison.

As he drifted from town to town, he stole what he needed to survive. Again, he resumed his quest to locate his long-lost son. As his nickel-and-dime thefts of food and clothing continued, his luck again ran out. Jack found himself visiting a half dozen jails over the next several years. Since none of the offenses were serious, he spent sort stints in an out of prison. After months and years of searching, he stumbled into a town where a freak show had performed recently.

Residents were still talking about the two young boys who toured the town, encouraging residents to attend the entertaining show. One of the boys from the Marvelous Marvels Touring Company was extremely tall, the other extremely short. When he sought additional descriptions, he realized the tiny teen might be Delbert. When residents described him, it was as if they were describing his beloved wife. He always thought the baby was a mirror image of his beloved Estar. Could he have just missed the opportunity to reunite with his son? He asked, and nobody knew where the carnival had gone except that they had headed south. So did Jack.

A year later, Elliott crossed over into Texas where he no longer was a wanted man. He'd never been to the Lone Star State. Again, he was destitute, though. He was without money to feed himself and he didn't believe anyone would hire a man like him. So, he went back to his thieving ways.

Even though he spent many years in prison and warmed cots in countless jails, Jack was still a nickel-and-dime crook. Except for his stolen horse and saddle —an offense akin to murder in Texas—he had never stolen anything of great value. He treated his horse with great respect, realizing if he lost his horse on the Texan plains, he might as well die.

He headed deeper south, where he guessed the weather was warmer. He was in East Texas and near the Gulf of Mexico which brought warmer temperatures to the arid land. He had long lost track of any possible movements of his only kin.

Although he longed to reunite with his son, he had reconciled to the fact it was not going to ever happen. As the months passed, he seemed to lose his way, drifting from one broken-down town to the next. He stole food from porches and windowsills. He often raided chicken coops for eggs or a choice hen. On his last endeavor, he received a backside full of buckshot for his efforts. Nonetheless, he got away with ten eggs. He cracked the eggs open as he walked and swallowed the slimy contents. Making fires on the trail was danger-ous, so he made cold camps and kept moving. Even without the sheriff on his heels, he felt like he was on the run all the time.

He had crossed Texas and was in El Paso when he finally realized he had been running away from himself. He got a job as a dishwasher and spittoon cleaner in a backstreet saloon. He was fed up with his wandering lifestyle and decided to end his life. Without his dignity and his only son—both of which were faint memories —he felt there was no more reason to live. One evening he spent his last coins on a bottle of whiskey, mounted his horse, and rode to the edge of town where a stand of oak trees grew. Some of them were lightning-racked and rotten, but Jack hardly noticed. He had drunk half the bottle of whiskey on his way there.

Upon his arrival, he cried out, "God, why have you forsaken me? What did I do to deserve such a life?"

It was true, he had lost his life in prison, his son to the consequences, and his honor over time. Now, he didn't even respect himself. What would his beloved Estar think of the way he had turned out? Nothing good had happened in his life since she passed away shortly after Delbert was born.

He tied a noose on one end of a rope and tossed the other end over a limb ten feet above his head. He knotted it and slipped the noose around his neck. A cascade of tears cut white paths down his cheeks as he thought about how he would never see his son again. Without Delbert, there was no sense in living.

"I'm sorry, Delbert!" Jack cried out as he kicked the flanks of the horse he had stolen a year earlier. The animal hesitated, kicked its hind feet, and then bolted. Jack easily slipped from the saddle and dropped toward the ground. Suddenly, the rope tightened around his neck. The coarse noose burned his neck as it cut off air to his lungs. He welcomed death.

Then, with a loud crash, the limb he used to hang himself broke. It crashed on top of his head and knocked him unconscious. When he awoke, he slowly sat upright, blinked his eyes, and rubbed the large knot on his skull. His shoulders shuddered hard, and the tears again flowed. BAD LUCK again had defied him and refused to let him end his life. He was such a failure he couldn't even kill himself successfully.

* * *

A FEW MONTHS LATER, Jack was working in a stable on the outskirts of El Paso. It was the side of town where the brothels, saloons, and gambling halls were plentiful. The stable owner frequently traded in stolen horses, a fact known by many but could never be proven.

The town marshal was an ex-gunfighter, a lawman on the rebound. Like Jack, the stable owner had spent time in prison and Jack soon considered him a friend. Eventually, Elliott accompanied his boss on night excursions across the border to steal Mexican horses. It was a common practice in South Texas. The horses were rebranded and sold to local cattlemen. Being the horses were not stolen in the United States, it was not a crime in Texas.

Just the same, one day the infamous marshal came to the stables with a Mexican rancher to confirm the theft. It just so happened the horses they had stolen belonged to an important Mexican rancher, who had connections on both sides of the border. Although technically it was not a crime, the stable owner was accused and taken into custody.

Jack hid in the hayloft until the marshal and rancher

left with his boss. Again, he ran for his life, assuming he was now a wanted man in Texas. He rode north into bad weather and across vast stretches of vacant land where nobody lived. He felt as though he had been running all his life and he was tired. So, with much soul searching, he made a difficult decision.

He decided to go to Big Spring and give himself up.

12. ANGUS MCGEE

Big Spring, Texas

ANGUS MCGEE HAD BEEN THE SHERIFF OF BIG SPRING for longer than he cared to remember. When he had been elected to the job, he hadn't intended to spend more than a year keeping law and order in the fledgling community.

Nearly ten years had passed, and he still sat at the same wooden desk, enjoying being lazy. He had grown a big belly and fat cheeks. It was cold and dreary outside, so he had stoked the cast-iron stove full of coal. Hazy waves of heat radiated out from the stove like ripples in a pond seeking out the corners of the wooden building and chasing off the chill. It was early and Angus had just awakened. He slept in the last cot in the cellblock, another reason he had stayed so long. With free room and board, a man would be hard-pressed to find a better situation. He was a man who had spent a lifetime being a marshal or a sheriff in small towns across Texas.

Sheriff McGee was a lawman long before he

wandered into Big Spring all those years ago. Back then, he was a US Marshal. He had grown tired of riding from one end of the country to the other, chasing down men who weren't worth his time.

Since arriving in Big Spring, there hadn't had much chasing to do, and he had yet to deal with a murder. So, year after year he was re-elected. As he was never sure he wanted to stay or not, he never campaigned nor made any effort to sway the votes one way or the other. He always felt if the town wanted a new sheriff, it mattered little to him. If he left, the only thing he would miss was a warm place to sleep and three meals a day. The pay was less than his last job, but he simply was too lazy to decide his future.

He wrapped his reading glasses around his ears, one at a time, and adjusted them just right. He picked up the envelope the mayor had hand-delivered the day before, pulled the piece of yellow paper from inside, and read it again. The words were right there before his eyes. He reread them and shook his head.

The communiqué informed him his service was no longer needed because the town had hired another man to take over his duties. He knew the end would come one day, but he was surprised by the form it had arrived on his desk. Such was the way of politics.

Big Spring had grown considerably since he had become the sheriff of what was once a small town. It appeared city leaders wanted a more educated man to hold the position. Today his job was more about collecting taxes than it was about catching the evil men who had once populated West Texas.

The state's violent times had passed, and Big Spring wanted a new image. He had briefly met the new sheriff.

He wore a fancy black suit that concealed the weapon he carried in a shoulder harness. That's right. The dandy kept a .22 caliber, five-shot revolver tucked away so as not to frighten the citizenry.

Of course, Angus carried his two double-action six-shooters on his hips, and another Colt Walker was pushed into his belt. The white bone handle of a knife was visible from one of his boots. In the old days, a well-armed lawman made outlaws think twice about taking aggressive measures. Often, just the presence of such an armory makes outlaws give themselves up. If shit hit the fan, a well-armed lawman had enough firepower to defend himself against more than one man with a gun. Eighteen bullets were preferable to five shots from a light-caliber weapon, which never would stop a determined outlaw from doing what he wanted.

McGee didn't believe in carrying pee shooters and never had. If he aimed his gun at a man and fired, he expected it to, at the very least, put him down, most times six feet under the ground. That was something a short-barreled, .22-caliber pistol wouldn't do. A well-placed shot in the eye might deter an outlaw if it was fired at point-blank range. Smaller pistols made it difficult to hit the broad side of a barn at thirty or forty feet. Anywhere else, a bullet or two of such a light caliber would not stop a determined man, especially if they were large.

When Sheriff McGee heard a soft knock at the door at such an early hour, he couldn't help but wonder who it could be on such a cold morning. Maybe it was that new dandy sheriff ready to send him on his way. Perhaps he was eager to take over the office. He frowned and felt distressed that his peaceful morning of reading the newspaper and drinking coffee was to be interrupted. Without another thought, he shoved the double deadbolts back and opened the door. A huge man stood out in the cold with his head down.

"Hurry up and get inside, mister. I don't want all the heat to escape my office," Angus said as he looked at the man from head to toe. He immediately noted the stranger wasn't armed. "You look like you're half frozen to death. Come on in, I ain't got all morning."

Jack Elliott mumbled, "Much obliged!" as he crossed the threshold, and the sheriff pushed the door closed against the freezing wind from a blizzard that had just passed. The temperatures were still below freezing. Ice was visible up and down the street, but the snow had finally stopped.

"Get on over there beside the pot-bellied stove and you'll thaw out in a few minutes, mister," the sheriff said. "You've got to get your toes and fingers warmed up or you'll get frostbite. You don't want to lose a digit or two."

Jack was so cold his teeth chattered like clucking hens. His coat was warm but traveling on foot much of the way from El Paso tested his willpower. His boots had holes in them. So, the cold shot up from the frozen ground and through his body. When he tried to tell the sheriff his name, he couldn't get the words out for his chattering teeth.

"Did you walk here through that blizzard, son? My name is Sheriff McGee, but everybody calls me Angus. Once you warm up and stop chattering, maybe you'll be able to tell me who you are and what I can do for ya."

The hard old lawman poured a tin cup to the brim

with boiling coffee and handed it to the hulking man. His eyes seemed to twinkle with some untold message.

"Here, get some of this hot java into ya. It'll get rid of the cold. You sure are a big one, ain't ya?"

It must have taken a full thirty minutes for the big fella to stop shivering enough to begin to get out a few words that the sheriff could understand. When he seemed ready to talk, the look of guilt cast a shadow over his face, one the lawman knew well.

"You come here to fess up to something, did ya?" Angus helped him to begin.

Sheriff McGee pulled on his long beard. It fell in white waves across his chest. He pushed his hat back with a puzzled look and waited patiently for the giant man to say whatever it was he wanted.

"Well, Sheriff," Jack said as he looked at the floor and stared at the toes of his boots. "I've come here to turn myself in."

"And what may I ask have you done wrong?" Angus asked and smiled. Jack saw the smile reach the lawman's eyes and calmed down slightly.

"I ain't gonna bite ya," Angus added. "So, go ahead and spit it out."

"My boss, back in El Paso. was arrested for rustlin' cattle," Jack said.

The sheriff's eyes narrowed as he now saw the crime may have been serious. In Texas, rustling horses was still a hanging violation. The admission made him more wary of the confessing man.

"And how are you involved?" Angus asked. "Did you steal the horses and cattle with him?"

"Yes, sir, I did," Jack replied honestly.

The sheriff grumbled some as he began to sort

through the wanted posters. There was a dozen from the US Marshal's Office on rustlers, but none of them described the man standing in front of him.

"I don't have anything here to speak of, son," Angus said, lost for an answer. "I best lock you up in cell number two so I can send a telegram to the law down in El Paso and wait until I hear further."

Elliot turned toward the sheriff and stuck out his hands as if he was expecting him to cuff and chain him as they had done in the other jails he had frequented. Instead, the sheriff just chuckled.

"Unless you tell me, you can outrun a bullet, I doubt handcuffs will be necessary, Jack." The sheriff snickered. "How about some breakfast before you get some rest? That is a hell of a long walk. I still don't know how you did it."

Jack's eyes returned to the floor, and he confessed, "I snuck into a couple of supply wagons some bull-whackers were drivin' but they didn't know I was in the back. We all got caught out in the storm. Those men seemed to smell their way north because, for a while, we traveled in a whiteout. I reckon if I hadn't stowed aboard, I would have frozen to death for sure."

"Well, I figure it's a good thing they didn't catch ya or they might have used those whips on ya. They don't take kindly to strangers taking free rides. Them boys be about making money. That's why they braved the storm like they did. If their cargo arrives late, they don't get paid.

"Sit down here at the table until your teeth stop chatterin' and I'll work up some frying pan biscuits and eggs. That'll put some more heat into your belly."

The last thing Jack had expected was for the sheriff

to be so generous. He was nothing like the guards and lawmen he had met in the past. Maybe Jack's old friend, BAD LUCK, was on vacation today.

* * *

TWO DAYS PASSED, and the new sheriff still hadn't taken over Angus McGee's job. He had come to the office several times, but he was so busy making speeches about all the things he was gonna do for the town, he hadn't yet had time to take over the day-to-day chores. So, the old sheriff sat and waited for the dandy to arrive, take his badge, and send him on his way.

In the meantime, he and the prisoner got to know each other a bit. After a few dozen games of checkers, Jack revealed all his past sins and hardships. Angus chuckled as he captured three of his checkers and crowned his king. In two more moves, he beat Jack for the umpteenth time.

"If I ever did hear a sad story, son, that be it," Angus huffed compassionately and waddled his head. "I know how hard this country can be. Sometimes a man has little choice as to what he does or doesn't do. Do you have any idea where your son is now? How are you going to find him if you don't know what he looks like? No offense or nothin', but having a father as big as you and a mother who was a midget might make it hard to figure out which way he's gone. I'm afraid you're lookin' for a needle in a haystack. How do you even know if you're lookin' in the right state?"

Two days later, he finally received a telegram back from the El Paso marshal. Sure enough, it stated Jack was a suspect in the theft of a few head of cattle and horses. The telegram also revealed the horses were rustled in Mexico, across the Rio Grande that marked the border between the two nations. So, Angus found himself between a rock and a hard place.

"Well, I ain't an expert on the law but one thing I know for sure is this," McGee said. "If you stole the cattle in Mexico, you ain't committed any crimes here in Texas. So, as far as I can see, you be a free man, Jack."

Elliot blinked his eyes in disbelief. He had been positive he was going back to prison or worse. In Texas, they hung horse thieves. Somehow, good fortune had blessed him yet again. The ever-suspicious man felt BAD LUCK had to be playing a trick on him. He had never caught a break in his life. Why should he be so lucky now?

"That can't be right," Jack said, amazed by the sheriff's revelation. "You mean I'm gettin' a break?"

"You don't get no breaks if you break the law, son. The fact is you didn't as far as I can see. I know the marshal back in El Paso. I used to work with the scoundrel. He's got his hands in so many pockets he's probably just doin' a favor for one of the Mexicans from across the river. As far as I'm concerned, you're as free as a bird."

"But where am I to go now?" Jack asked, still bewildered.

"Once this new-fangled sheriff takes over the office, I'm headin' for Abilene, Texas. That's just two towns over but it's the hub for cattle shipments across the country. If there's a job to be had, I figure it'll be there. Have ya ever considered being a deputy sheriff?"

Jack was so shocked by the question he nearly fell

off his chair. This got a big belly laugh from the weathered marshal. His worn eyes twinkled even more.

"You'd be surprised how many men outside the law end up being a sheriff or a marshal. The marshal in El Paso himself has spent time in jail," Angus explained. "Hell, look at men like Wild Bill Hickock or Wyatt Earp. Both of them would be villains in any other state but this one. Here they are working as lawmen. Hell, Earp was even arrested a few times himself in Tombstone after that big shoot-out they had with Doc Holliday and the Clantons.

"Shit, you'd be no different, and you don't have half the baggage those two got. Why don't ya come along with me and we can partner up? A big fella like you'd make a fine deputy. There'd be few buckaroos who wouldn't want to mess with the likes of you, son."

"What about my criminal past?" Jack asked.

"Don't you think you've suffered enough for one lifetime, amigo?" Angus asked. "My lips are sealed—to that I'll swear. Plus, the things you have done since you were railroaded don't amount to much of any serious crimes in my book. You've never hurt a person, have ya? Have ya shot anyone?"

"I hurt a few in that Louisiana pen, but I ain't killed nobody," he admitted.

That doesn't count because you were just tryin' to survive while doin' time for a crime you didn't commit," McGee reasoned.

"Good," Jack said.

No sooner did Jack begin to consider his future, the snooty new sheriff showed up to inform McGee he was moving in the following day. He also asked what offense the prisoner had committed. Angus lied and said vagrancy.

"He's done his three days, so he's free to go. I reckon that makes two of us now, don't it?"

The city dandy stood by the door, tapping his foot impatiently. Then he proclaimed, "I expect to come here tomorrow morning at nine and find you and the prisoner, gone. Is that clear, McGee?"

"Well, as most sheriffs get up with the roosters, I figure we'll be long gone by then."

McGee sucked on a wad of tobacco and spat a stream of brown juice a yard long at the feet of the man in fancy duds. It was clear there was little respect between the two. The fancy new sheriff thought him above everyone else and the old lawman knew a fool when he saw one.

13. SURPRISE REUNION

Big Spring, Texas

MUCH TO SHERIFF MCGEE'S SURPRISE, THE NEXT morning when he opened his eyes, a dim light came from the table by the stove. The lantern was lit with the wick turned down low. As he pulled his boots on and slipped his red suspenders over his shoulders, he smiled. The smell of hot coffee, frying eggs, and bacon filled the sheriff's office.

"I figured if we had to move on today, the least I could do is make you breakfast, sheriff," Jack said.

"You don't have to call me sheriff anymore, Jack. From now on, just call me Angus like all my friends do."

The two were just wiping their plates clean with pieces of fresh bread from a hot loaf when they heard a scratching sound at the door. Out of old habit, Angus moved his hand toward the handle of his revolver.

"This ain't the time for visits," Angus whispered and waved his hand for Jack to stand out of the way. The big man moved into the shadows and waited for whatever was to come.

Then, somebody knocked on the door. Over the years, a lawman becomes accustomed to the knocks from different kinds of men. The city dandy who was to take over for the sheriff rapped at the door with a hooked index finger—kind of like a woman. An outlaw or a hard lawman knocked hard like they were always angry. Angus was pretty sure this was the knock of a child. He looked at Jack and moved his hand away from his gun.

When the door opened Angus was confronted by two boys. One was the biggest youngster he'd ever seen. The other was small, about the size of a ten-year-old.

"We came to have a word with you, Sheriff," the small one stammered as his teeth chattered from the cold.

"Well, don't stand out there freezing to death. Come on in and warm yourselves by the fire. But you'll have to be quick. We were just leaving, and I'm afraid I ain't the sheriff no more."

The look of disappointment was unmistakable on the boys' faces. The sheriff appeared to have said exactly what they didn't want to hear.

The sheriff smiled his warmest and said, "Don't worry so. Tell me what it is botherin' ya."

That was when the Tonkawa cousins stepped up behind Del and Tommy. This wasn't the plan Potak had laid out for them. So, the boys were just as surprised as the sheriff.

"Well, I'll be damned, I ain't see you two old birds in ten years," Angus McGee said. "I thought you'd both be dead by now."

"Howdy, Sheriff," Potak said with a grin.

Tuc made a face like he wanted to cut his throat and growled, "We had hoped you'd be dead too." The weathered warrior shot daggers at the old lawman.

"Well, first of all, I ain't a lawman no more," Angus replied as his eyes twinkled with mischief. "You see a badge? Now, there ain't no reason to hold grudges about things that happened a decade ago. Hell, I never did throw you two in jail anyway, now did I?"

"You threatened us enough times," Potak said and snickered. "You also threatened to shoot us."

"You know I can't read what it says on your badge," Tuc snapped, suddenly angry. This startled both Del and Tommy.

But apparently, Potak felt it was time to let bygones be bygones.

"We come in peace, McGee," Potak said. "We are helping these two boys."

"Since when do you two be trackin' for youngsters?" Angus asked. "I thought you worked for the Texas Rangers?"

"That was a long time ago, too," Potak replied with old eyes.

"Come on in already or we're gonna lose all the heat from the coal burner," the jolly lawman said.

Once they all got into the warm room the two boys stood before the sheriff, shifting their weight from one foot to the other. They were as nervous as a polecat in hunting season.

"Well, come out with it then," Angus said and waited patiently.

Delbert hesitated like he was scared to ask. Then he just blurted it out, "We're lookin' for somebody."

"Well, I'll be." Angus laughed. "You hear that, Jack? These fellas be looking for someone, just like you is. The world has gone mad, now ain't it?"

"The world is full of fools," Tuc grumbled.

Angus squinted one eye toward Tuc and said, "That be a fact, you old blackbird." He spat another long stream of juice into an empty peach tin he had in his hand, smiled, and said, "And how are you two mixed up in all this?"

That was when Jack came out of the shadows and laid eyes on the visitors. He hadn't seen such a collection of misfits since he fled Ichabod Justice's Touring Company some fifteen years ago. Two White boys, one small and the other taller than him, were flanked by two ancient Indians. He wondered what business the unlikely foursome had with the sheriff on such a cold day.

First, he looked at the huge boy. For an instant, he hoped he might recognize him. When his eyes shifted to the smaller one, his heart jumped into his throat, and color drained from his face.

Images of his beloved wife, Estar, flashed through his sluggish brain. Her dark eyes smiled at him just before she took her last breath so many years ago. The same eyes were looking up at him now. He couldn't move.

"I must be dreaming," he whispered, loud enough for all to hear.

"Do you believe dreams can come true, Jack?" Potak asked.

"Yes...no...well, I don't know," the hulking man said as he looked from the medicine man to the sheriff and then back at the small boy. "All my dreams turn into nightmares."

"What did you dream of last night?" Tuc asked.

"I dreamed about my late wife and the son I've never known. It's the same dream I've had for years. Who are you people, how did you know my name and why have you come here?" Jack asked, his eyes focusing on the smallest person.

Then there was silence. The wind howled outside and a nearby tree, coated with ice, groaned as a giant limb broke off and crashed onto the snowy alleyway behind the jail.

"My name is Delbert Elliott," the little teen said. "These are my friends. We've come a long way to find a father I never knew," he said in a high-pitched voice. "This is my best friend, Tommy, and our Tonkawa friends, Potak and Tuc.

"No, it can't be," Jack said and fell to his knees. His hands covered his face as tears spilled from his eyes. "I don't deserve this."

"It is I who did not deserve to be abandoned," the sixteen-year-old teen said. His voice was still high-pitched but it had conviction in it. "If there is still no room in your heart for me, we will leave you here; I've gotten along just fine without a father in my life."

Again, there was silence. All eyes were on the big man who kneeled and sobbed on the floor.

Delbert yanked Tommy's sleeve and said, "Let's go. Maybe you'll have better luck with your mother."

Tuc's mouth became a fierce gash, his fingers slid to his knife, and he muttered under his breath. Potak rested a hand on his arm to restrain him.

That's when Jack realized his dream had become true. He leaped to his feet and raced to his son. He swept him up into his arms, spun him around, and cried out, "Thank you, Lord. I promise I will sin no more."

Next, he fell to his knees, placed his son's feet back on the ground, and held him at arm's length. Delbert was the spitting image of his mother. He was convinced destiny finally had smiled upon him.

Jack used his sleeve to wipe tears from his eyes and said, "Thank you for finding me, Delbert. I have dreamed of this day for years. When I lost your mother, I thought I had lost everything. I looked everywhere for you, but it was hard to find you from a jail cell, and I've seen the inside of far too many.

"Until this moment, my life has been nothing but misery. Now you fill me with joy and hope. I feel like a new man. If you'll let me, I'd like to start over. I promise to be the father you deserve and the one your mother expected me to be. Will you give me a second chance?"

"I thought you hated me," Del said, holding back the joy that was turning his stomach upside down.

"No, I hated myself," Jack said.

The tiny teen looked up at Potak. Then he glanced at Tuc. Finally, he looked at his partner and best friend, Tommy. He still was shivering from their icy trek to the sheriff's office. The tall teen winked at his friend and nudged him forward.

When Del looked back toward his father, Jack was shaking, too, but with heartfelt emotion.

"I knew you couldn't hate me. Look at me, Pop. I'm short, but I'm damn near perfect in every other way."

Then, he leaped forward and threw his arms around Jack's neck, and said, "I'm going to hold you to your promise, too."

"Well, ain't this the darndest thing you've ever seen,"

McGee said to his two Indian friends. "Them two couldn't be any happier if they were dipped in chocolate."

When Angus leaned his head back to laugh, his big white beard raised off his chest and his belly shook as if it was chock-full of Miss Hutchins's strawberry jam.

Potak looked at his cousin and said, "We still have work to do."

* * *

THE SIX NEW and old acquaintances cleaned out the sheriff's store of breakfast supplies as they celebrated the warm reunion of father and son.

With a full belly, the sheriff leaned back in his chair, looked at the two old Indians, and asked, "Where are you two old coots off to now?"

"We are almost at the end of our quest," Tuc said.

"What kind of quest might that be? You still hunting Comanche scalps?"

"I have room for a few more," Tuc said as he stroked a scalp sewn into his buckskin shirt. "They are hard to come by these days."

"Our mission is peaceful," Potak explained. "Now that we have located the small boy's father, we search for the tall boy's mother."

"What's her name?" the sheriff asked.

"Emily Turnbolt, but I just called her M," Tommy blurted out. "Maybe you've heard of her."

"No, I'm sorry to say that name doesn't ring a bell," McGee said.

"I know that name," Jack interjected, looking from

his son to Tommy. "Was your mother the bearded lady in Justice's sideshow?"

"Yes!" Tommy replied, excited to hear Jack remembered his mother.

"She was an odd sort, but got pregnant about the time Estar did," Jack added. "This all is starting to make sense. The two of you have to be about the same age."

"We've been best friends forever," Del said. "Jack's mother was kidnapped just before his tenth birthday. We haven't seen her since. That's why we're looking for her now."

"Hell's bells, boys, you might as well dip me in chocolate now," the sheriff said with another big belly laugh. "I hear tell there's a bearded woman tending bar at the Buckhorn Gentlemen's Club in Abilene. And it just so happens that's where we were headin'. You're welcome to join us."

Everyone but Tommy was smiling. Suddenly, he had become silent and withdrawn. Delbert noticed his massive hands were clenched tight and trembling ever so slightly.

"Don't worry, Tommy. We're going to find her, and she's going to be happy to see you," Delbert assured.

14. THE BEARDED BEAUTY

Somewhere outside Kansas City

EMILY TURNBOLT WAS SUBJECTED TO MONTHS OF ABUSE after she was kidnapped from the Marvelous Marvels Touring Company. Her tale of woe only began when two drunken cowboys stole her from her tent on the outskirts of Kansas City.

The Pistol brothers, Clint and Rory, had arrived in Kansas City behind a herd of three hundred Longhorn steers that were being driven north out of Texas. Americans east and west could not get enough Texas beef to satisfy their needs, and ranches made big money by driving their herds to the stockyards and shipping cattle east and west.

When the Rocking R drovers reached their destination and were paid for their services, the only thing on the brothers' minds was whiskey and women. They had already finished half a bottle of whiskey when they came upon Ichabod Justice's troupe of misfits and performers.

They had money in their pockets and were looking to have a good time. What better way than to take a gander at a caravan full of misfits and oddities? Of course, the bearded lady with the picture-perfect figure was their favorite attraction.

They followed a dozen onlookers behind the canvas curtain five times to ogle the shapely performer. Emily noticed the brothers immediately because they were young and enthusiastic. They whistled and clapped every time she entered and exited the stage.

By her fourth appearance, they had worked their way to the front row and were more exuberant than any of the other customers. She realized they were drunk but didn't care. As long as they kept dropping a dime for admission, she would wiggle and tantalize.

The brothers were disappointed when she leaned over and let an old timer pull on her whiskers. When she flashed her cleavage in their faces and winked at them, common sense went out the window.

Outside the performer's tent, the brothers debated whether to spend one more dime for a chance to pull on the woman's beard. Clint didn't believe it was real, and Rory wanted to find out if it was.

"It's all an act to entice us to spend our hard-earned money," explained Clint, the oldest of the two brothers. "You know that beard ain't real. No woman can grow whiskers."

"But she's beautiful," impressionable and drunken Rory said. "I keep thinking about how soft that beard is going to feel when she lets me grab a hold of it."

"You're drunker than I thought," Clint replied. "We're out of whiskey. Let's head back into town."

"Nope! Not yet. I know if we pay one more dime,

she'll let me tug on them whiskers. She knows I'm smitten by her. Didn't you see her wink at me?"

"She winks at all the customers, stupid," Clint said. "That's why cowboys like us plunk down a dime for a peek."

"I'll prove you wrong, big brother. Come on. This trip inside is on me," Rory said and handed two more dimes to the enterprising caravan owner who was taking admission and encouraging passersby to see "The World's Most Beautiful Bearded Lady."

The fifth trip behind the Marvelous Marvels curtain was a charm for Rory Pistol.

Emily Turnbolt danced and pranced across the stage, stopping at intervals to smile and tease customers with her uncommon beauty. The beard was blonde and covered both cheeks and lay in waves of curls on the top of her chest. She wore a fashionable gown that plunged to reveal considerable cleavage. As she danced across the stage, she played a merry tune on a fiddle.

Occasionally, she would stop and engage customers. When she didn't wear her hair in a long braid, she stepped before a wall-hung mirror and ran a large comb through her golden locks, which stretched almost to her waist. As she performed the task, the audience was transfixed on the satin that stretched across and hugged her firm backside. She knew exactly how to move her hips to entice male onlookers and flaunt their desire.

When she turned suddenly from the mirror to face her audience, she smiled fetchingly and ran the comb through the waves of whiskers. Her sultry moves somehow made the presence of female whiskers seem as natural as sunshine on a Missouri day.

Next, she pranced and danced playfully across the stage one more time and stopped directly in front of the Pistol brothers. Rory was hooting and whistling the loudest. She dropped to her knees, wiggled her shoulders enticingly, and offered up her whiskers for Rory to test.

The nineteen-year-old Texan suddenly went silent, mesmerized by the woman's ample bosom, green eyes, and ruby lips. He didn't even notice as she pushed her chin closer so he could prove to the crowd they were real.

Clint elbowed him in the ribs and said, "Wake up, stupid! Now is the chance you have been waiting for."

"Go ahead, handsome. Show the crowd my beard is real," Emily said in a deep, sultry voice.

Slowly Rory raised his hands to the woman's face. He wrapped his fingers in the long, soft whiskers and smiled. Then, he pulled her forward and kissed her flush on the lips. His actions caught Emily off guard. If not for Clint's quick actions, she might have toppled forward and off the stage. Clint stepped in and made sure she wasn't hurt.

Ever the performer, Emily tried to act unfazed by the drunken cowboy's unexpected and affectionate reaction. "Thank you," she said to Clint and cast angry eyes at his drunken brother. "I'm glad there is one gentleman in the crowd."

She concluded her performance by inviting the onlookers back for her sixth and final appearance of the day. "I always like to end the day with a song. Won't you come back and join me?" she said with a broad smile and sashayed off the stage.

Justice was waiting for her when she walked off the stage and saw the anger in her eyes.

"Don't allow those two in for my last show, Ichabod. I won't be manhandled by any man," she ordered and stormed away.

* * *

THE PISTOL BROTHERS did not return for the sixth show. They headed back to the Sagebrush Saloon for more whiskey and fun. After being tantalized by the shapely bearded beauty, Clint was ready to be entertained by one of the establishment's sporting gals.

"I don't know about you, brother, I'm ready for a real poke," he said. "I've had my fill of marvels and sideshow freaks."

"She weren't no freak!" Rory declared as he sipped his whiskey. "I bet she's a better poke than any of these fat cows."

"Well, the difference is these cows are willing; your bearded enchantress is not. Granted, she's got all the right curves, but she gives me the creeps. I could not believe you kissed her. Why would you kiss a woman with whiskers?"

"Watch your mouth, brother. You kiss who you want, and I'll kiss who I want. You go on and take care of whatever business and pleasure you desire. I'll be waiting here for you when you finish up."

Clint's moment of pleasure lasted for less than fifteen minutes. When he returned to the table where his brother sat, Rory was still sipping whiskey and staring out into the empty street. He paid little attention as his brother expounded about the pleasing attributes of the female anatomy.

A few more painted ladies came by their table and tried to coax the brothers upstairs for another rendezvous, but they refused. Rory got angry when they were propositioned by a rather obnoxious working gal.

"I kissed an angel today. Why would I want to stoop so low to couple with a cow like you? Leave us alone," he growled.

They drank alone for another hour, never exchanging another word. Both men were lost in the reverie of female magnetism, one imaginary and the other post-coital.

Following Clint's second trip upstairs with one of the soiled doves, Rory made a proclamation: "I'm going to rescue my beloved from that sideshow. She should come with us back to Texas."

Clint was beyond drunk and surprised his brother when he agreed and said, "You may be right, little brother. Shave that beard off her, and I might give her a poke, too."

Rory pulled his Colt, tapped it against his brother's chest, and said, "No you won't!"

"I was just k-kidding m-man," Clint said and held his hands high in the air.

"Don't kid no more!"

"All right! You want her; let's go get her," Clint said. Both brothers were too drunk to think straight, let alone get involved in a kidnapping. Of course, alcohol never did improve the thought process.

* * *

WHEN THE PISTOL BROTHERS entered the tent that belonged to the "World's Most Beautiful Bearded Lady," they found the woman and a young boy sound asleep. They stuffed bandanas into the mouths of their victims as they slept. Then, they hogtied their ankles as if they were roping calves on the open range.

The young boy, Tommy, was big for his age but easily controlled by Clint. Then, he rushed to help his brother who had his hands full with the bearded woman. She was fighting for her very life. In his drunken state, Rory was having difficulty getting control of her wrists. Every time he got close to her, she scratched and clawed like a hellcat.

Clint didn't hesitate. He slammed his Army Colt against her temple, and she collapsed unconscious. Rory wasted no time. He pulled a nightdress over her head and tore at her undergarments as spittle formed in the corner of his mouth.

"I'm going to show you what a real lady looks like, big brother," he said as his eyes grew to the size of silver dollars. When the brothers saw her in the flesh, sans clothes, they both gasped. She was the most beautiful thing they had ever seen.

"Holy Mother of God," Clint said as he marveled at the gentle curves and full figure. "You were right, little brother. Now, I want to see what she looks like without that beard."

As she lay unconscious, one brother took advantage of her and the other used his razor-sharp Bowie to shave away her whiskers. By the time, Rory was sated, Clint had removed most of her blonde facial hair. She looked completely different and more beautiful than either of the brothers had ever imagined.

"What do you want to do with her now?" Clint asked.

"She's comin' with us back to Texas to be my woman," Rory proclaimed.

"Are you crazy?" his brother asked.

"No, I'm in love," Rory said.

"You don't know the first thing about love," Clint whispered defiantly.

"That's what you say," Rory said smartly.

He stripped the blanket out from under the unconscious woman, wrapped her in it, and hoisted her over his shoulder.

"Come on! Let's go!" he ordered.

"Wait! What about the kid?" Clint asked.

"Leave him here. He's big enough to get along on his own," Rory said and strolled hastily for the exit.

They didn't realize Tommy was only nine years old, and it was a night he would never forget.

THE PISTOL BROTHERS, with their stolen prize wrapped in a blanket, left Kansas City in a hurry and under the cover of darkness. They rode west aboard two sturdy mustangs and with Emily tied to a third horse that was tethered to Rory's saddle horn. They were an hour away before the sun began to creep over the far horizon. The kidnapping had brought the brothers out of their drunken stupor. They knew they had to get as far away as they could if they were going to successfully transport the woman to Texas.

Depravity overwhelmed them, though. Each time they stopped to rest their horses, the brothers took turns at Emily. Soon she quit fighting and just let them have their way. Her beloved beard was gone. So was her child and her will to live.

Less than one hundred miles west of Kansas City, the brothers were set upon by a hunting party of Plains Indians. They were a bitter horde because they were heading to their winter home knowing the great buffalo herds that had sustained their tribe for generations were no more. The White man had hunted them to near extinction.

They easily overwhelmed the brothers, who never saw them approaching. As they tortured them for the deeds of their brethren, the native women went through their belongings in search of valuables. When they came across the battered White woman wrapped in a bloody blanket, all gasped. She was covered in cuts and bruises from her cheeks to her thighs.

Keya, a strong-willed woman who was half Comanche and half Arapaho, immediately reported her findings to her husband, Chief Mathó Wanáȟtaka. He was overseeing the torture of the brothers when she whispered in his ear. Suddenly, the chief ordered the torture to stop. His order was far from a reprieve, though. Wanáȟtaka pulled his knife and marched toward the brothers with dark and deadly eyes. They howled in agony as he severed their privates, first Clint and then Rory. They bled out before other body parts were taken as souvenirs.

As the Indians prepared to leave the dead brothers hanging as a warning to all White hunters, the women treated Emily's wounds and placed her on a travois to be transported to their winter village in the mountains.

Emily spent two years in the Arapaho village, a slave

to the chief and his wife. She worked hard, learned to speak their language, and became an integral part of the village. As her beard grew back, however, all stayed away from her, fearing some evil spirit resided within her.

The Indians had never seen a woman with facial hair. Half feared her and the rest simply wanted to do away with her. A medicine man said Emily was a sign the White man was cursed. "As long as she lives, so shall the curse," their spiritual leader revealed. "Soon we will get our lands back from these evil White people who are half-man and half-woman."

It was not the White man who was cursed, though; it was all the native tribes. Eventually, all would be driven from their lands and forced to live on reservations.

When the Blue Coats came and slaughtered the village, they were shocked to find a blonde, White woman chanting over a fire and wrapped in a buffalo robe.

When Sergeant William Billingsley pulled her to her feet, he spoke to her in the first English words Emily had heard in two years. She was stunned for a moment, numb from the sight of the senseless murder of a peaceful people and the sound of her native tongue.

The sergeant was stunned when the woman turned to him and he saw her face was covered in blonde hair.

"Good god, who are you? What are you? How long have you been held captive by these savages?" he asked.

"You are the savages," she said. "These people have done nothing to harm you. Why would you senselessly kill everyone?"

"The hostiles have been raiding all over the territory.

We can't allow that. Come with me. Lieutenant Donald will have to deal with you."

Thus, began the next chapter in Emily Turnbolt's life. She was returned to civilization.

15. THE GENTLEMEN'S CLUB

At a fort near Abilene, Texas

ONCE EMILY WAS TAKEN INTO THE CUSTODY OF THE US Army, she was treated like a rotten potato nobody wanted. As Lieutenant Wesley Donald escorted her across the parade grounds in her buckskin apparel, she was mocked and ridiculed by the soldiers.

She was used to being gawked at. After all, she made good money working for Ichabod Justice. But the heathens at the military installation were worse than the drunken cowboys who kidnapped her. She could see hatred and scorn in their eyes. They assumed she was an Indian lover, and that made her more of a pyuria than her golden beard.

Lieutenant Donald had nothing but scorn for her when she was placed in his custody. "How many warrior beds did you warm, Indian lover?" he asked.

"It's none of your business, baby killer. Do not talk to me," she replied.

"What did you call me?"

"I called you what you are. There was no reason for your men to senselessly kill the women and children of that village. You are vermin," she replied and spat at his feet.

The lieutenant laughed and said, "You are going to find out Texans don't take kindly to your kind. Freaks like you don't belong in civilization."

Emily abruptly stepped toward him and slapped the man's face.

Angry, Donald's hand immediately went to his sword. His knuckles turned white as he considered running her through with the blade. He restrained himself and dragged her off to his commander's office.

"I'll be laughing when the colonel sets you free. You'll find no home in Texas. You will be scorned wherever you choose to go, and I'll make sure of it!"

When they entered the commander's office, Colonel Christopher Walker was so shocked by the sight of the bearded Indian woman he spit coffee across the top of the desk.

"What in tarnation?" he barked while trying to clean up his mess.

"Sir, let me introduce Miss Emily Turnbolt," Donald said. "She was a prisoner of the natives we disposed of a few days ago. She will be included in the report I submit forthwith. I thought it best to bring her here for you to deal with. She is as jaded and contrary as she is horrible to look at. I felt you would know what was best as she transitions back into civilization.

"As you can see, she is not your ordinary White woman. She's certainly not like any of the others I have rescued. She has been indoctrinated into the native culture but speaks English. It's her appearance that is most disgusting for the men, sir."

"I can imagine," Colonel Walker stated. "You are dismissed, Lieutenant. I will discuss Miss Turnbolt's future with her, and I look forward to your report."

When Donald saluted and left the office, Walker urged Emily to take a seat.

"Pardon me for my despicable reaction when you walked into the room, ma'am," he said. "As you must be aware, your appearance can be unsettling."

"I have no idea what you are talking about," she replied smartly. "The Arapaho had no problem with my appearance. They treated me far better than your soldiers."

"Were any of my men inappropriate toward you, ma'am?" he asked with a raised brow.

"I find killing women and children inappropriate. Your men's actions were as despicable as you," she barked.

Walker's face turned red, and he rose from his chair and glared at the woman. "The Indians have slaughtered families all across this territory," he declared. "They get what they deserve, no more and no less."

She laughed at him and said, "You have taken their land and altered their lifestyle by killing off all the buffalo in Texas. I understand the next step is annihilation of an entire race of people. Do you call that civilized behavior?"

"I call it R-E-V-E-N-G-E!" he shouted, seething with anger.

When he calmed and reclaimed his seat, the commander continued. "I apologize for my outburst, Miss Turnbolt, but I take my work here very seriously. I am going to remand you to our outfit's physician. Dr. Longstreet will see that you are healthy enough to return to civilization. I wish you well."

Walker called his clerk into his office and ordered him to escort Emily to the surgeon's quarters. He did reluctantly.

Emily found Ebenezer Longstreet more amicable than the colonel. Perhaps it was because he was a bit tipsy. She could smell alcohol on his breath.

Like the colonel, he was surprised to be confronted by a bearded woman but accustomed to seeing human deformity. He found it mysterious more than alarming.

"Have you always had facial hair?" he asked.

"For as long as I can remember," she replied.

"Even as a child?"

"Yes!"

"It is very odd, as you know," he added. "Nonetheless, I find it clean and charming in the way it falls to your chest in waves and curls. Most of the beards I see are filthy and bug infested."

"I'm not surprised," she replied indifferently. "What are you going to do with me? The colonel said I am your responsibility. You should know, I need no one to care for me. I will be fine."

"I think I will present you to Miss Lilly Townsend in Abilene. She runs a house for women. I assume you will fit in there and she can provide you with some of the commodities you will need to re-enter society."

"What on earth are you talking about?" Emily asked.

"I'm assuming you will be more than happy to shed your deerskin clothing for a dress and parasol, of course. We have none of those things here. Miss Lilly does, though," the doctor said.

"I don't think so," Emily replied, only to be contrary. The buckskins she wore were warm and comfortable. However, she thought back to the fine dresses she wore when she performed for Ichabod's touring company and smiled inwardly.

"I'm sure she can assist you in shaving your beard, too," Longstreet said.

"I will not!"

"You will not what?" he asked.

"I will not shave off my beard," she said indignantly.

"Well, that will be between you and Miss Lilly. We will leave first thing in the morning. I will leave you here to freshen up. There is a cot in the back room where you may rest. I must make my rounds at the infirmary. As you know, some of the soldiers were injured in the attack on the Arapaho village. I'll need to attend to their wounds."

"Heathens!" she blurted out.

"What?"

"Those men are savages! Do you not wonder why no soldiers were killed?" Emily asked.

"It was a miracle."

"No, the village was full of women, children, and old men, who were killed mercilessly. Most of the warriors were off hunting buffalo, which are becoming almost impossible to find in this territory."

"Oh my, how unfortunate," the doctor said, not wanting to get into a debate over the actions of the military. "Make yourself at home. I will return soon."

* * *

THE SUN SHONE brightly when Emily and the doctor pulled up to the railing in front of the two-story house in Abilene, she was impressed with its exterior. The house was whitewashed and surrounded by a white picket fence. It had a grand porch that wrapped around two sides and a massive entryway that was painted purple. A large sign in the front yard read: "Buckhorn Gentlemen's Club."

When the doctor knocked at the door, a tall, matronly-looking woman answered. She was dressed in a fine gown, wore gaudy jewelry, and her cheeks and lips were painted bright red.

"Why, hello, Dr. Longstreet," she said brightly. "I did not expect to see you this day. Is it time for your monthly visit already?"

Longstreet blushed and replied, "Oh, no. I've come seeking your assistance."

It was an odd statement for the military man, who once a month did health checks in Abilene.

"How so?" she asked.

"Well, the men rescued a White woman who had been held captive by the Arapaho. She has no family that I know of and requires a place to settle so she can re-enter society. The fort is no place for a woman. I thought you might be able to accommodate her needs quite easily."

Lilly looked over his shoulder at the woman seated in his carriage and said, "Oh my. She may be a project."

"Yes, but I know you will be able to help her," he said and beckoned for Emily to join him on the threshold of the large home.

Lilly raised her hand to her lips to muffle her surprise when she saw Emily's long beard. She composed herself quickly and said, "Come in, my dear. The doctor said you require a helping hand. I should say so. Fortunately, we never turn away a beautiful woman in distress."

Emily smiled shyly as she examined the elaborate interior décor. A large chandelier hung from a vaulted ceiling in the vestibule. Large rooms to the left and right were decorated in plush velvet and satin that was rich in color.

There was a hint of cigar smoke in the air, but it was the aroma of bacon frying somewhere in the expansive house that made Emily's stomach churn.

"I'm sure a warm bath and a dress will do you wonders, but shall we have breakfast first?" Lilly said. She placed her hands on Emily's shoulders, spun her around, and examined her from head to toe.

"Ah, yes," she added. "You have a fabulous figure, but it appears those Indians must have starved you to death. Come with me. We'll start putting some meat on those bones forthwith. The men who frequent my parlor prefer substance."

Suddenly, it dawned on Emily what kind of place she had been taken. It was a bordello.

* * *

WHEN THE TWO women entered the kitchen, a large Black woman hovered over a wood stove. She had bacon and eggs in a frying pan and hot grits warming in a pot.

"Breakfast almost ready, Miss Lilly," Lula, the cook, said. "I'll put a couple more eggs on for your guest. We've got plenty of grits and bacon."

When Lulu noticed the bearded woman, she dropped the spoon into the grits. They splashed and sizzled atop the hot stove. Her eyes grew the size of pie plates and she said without restraint, "Lordy be, I've seen it all now."

"This is Emily Turnbolt," Miss Lilly announced. "She doesn't look like much now. When we get her cleaned up, she'll shine like a bright new penny."

Lulu placed two plates in front of the women and said without hesitation, "I can see under them whiskers is a fine beauty, Miss Lilly. Get rid of them and you got yourself a prize gal."

"I don't plan on getting rid of my beard," Emily said bluntly. She looked at Lulu and then questioningly at her host.

"I reckon Miss Lilly has somethin' to say about that," Lulu said, shook her head, and trudged back to the stove, where she pulled biscuits from a Dutch oven.

Emily looked at her host with defiance and said, "Say whatever is on your mind. I've heard it all."

"The men who seek comfort from our girls will find your beard unattractive, dear. We most certainly will have to remove it," Lilly confessed.

"First, I'm not one of your girls," Emily said emphatically. "Second, you have no idea how appealing a bearded woman can be to men. How many have you known?"

"You are the first, most certainly."

The woman was kind enough to rescue her from the Army, so Emily revealed her affiliation with the Marvelous Marvels Touring Company and how hundreds—maybe thousands—of men had paid just to look at her.

"I may be able to do the same here, but I won't spread my legs for every man who happens to find me attractive," she said.

"I will give you the benefit of doubt," Lilly said. "We will see how attractive you are once we get you cleaned up. Know this, though, every woman who lives here earns her keep."

"I understand," Emily said, "and I appreciate your kindness. You should know, I don't take charity. If I cannot earn my keep, I'll be the first to move on."

Miss Lilly marveled at how confident the woman was. When she shed her buckskins, applied some makeup, and was adorned in a blue satin gown that showed off her wide shoulders and shapely figure, the club owner was astounded by her strange beauty. She found a place serving drinks behind the club's main bar. Emily was like the fine wine served at an elaborate dinner. Everybody wanted some, even though she wasn't available.

Men came from far and wide to enjoy the entertainment at the Buckhorn Gentlemen's Club. They always had a good time. But it was the blonde beauty with green eyes and a golden beard who stood out in a room filled with beautiful women. It mattered not that her beard fell across her bosom in waves and curls. Every man who left the club raved about the amazing bartender with the golden beard.

Emily felt like her life was back to normal.

Miss Lilly was pleased, too. She smiled every time she saw her bearded star entertaining a group of cowboys at the bar, where profits promptly tripled.

16. THE FINAL QUEST

Off to Abilene, Texas

WHEN THE GROUP OF UNLIKELY COMPANIONS LEFT THE sheriff's office, the snow again had stopped and a bright yellow sun broke through the clouds. Rays of light sparkled like tiny stars on the field of fresh snow beside the town livery.

"Come on," Angus said as he pushed forward through a foot of snow. Not a footprint could be seen; everything was white. Even the trees were snow-covered. The cold sky was winter blue, though. As they trudged through the snow, clouds of vapor came with every breath. Everyone was smiling, except Tuc who rarely broke a grin.

"I got a friend in the stables that'll loan us a two-team carriage," Angus said. "I'll make travel a mite more practical. It ain't got a roof, but it's mighty fast. We can tow my old Nelly behind us." He patted his fat belly and chuckled. "She don't like long trips since I've put on a pound or three. If I remember right, you two old birds don't take much to riding horses anymore either."

"If you move too fast, you miss too much," Potak replied. "When you walk, you miss little. Everyone is in too much of a hurry."

"How would you like it if a man rode on your back all day?" Tuc asked. "Have you ever caught a wild horse that wanted to be ridden?"

"How far is it to Abilene? Jack Elliot asked.

"It ain't but a stone's throw," McGee replied. "It's just over one hundred miles as the crow flies."

"How long will that take us?" Del asked.

With a buckboard wagon, you might do it in three or four days but with my partner's two-team buggy, we can do it in half the time.

The buggy turned out to be everything Angus promised and more. It had two bench seats with springs and the wheel spokes were painted yellow. It was as fancy a buggy Tuc and Potak had ever ridden.

"Wow!" Tommy said. "This must be one of the fastest buggies in Texas."

Angus manned the reins and Jack sat to his left with little Del in the middle. They put Tommy in the middle in the back so the wagon did not lean too far to one side. He sat between the Tonkawa. He had overcome his fear for Potak, but Tuc was another matter. Danger seemed to come from every pore of the bitter man.

Once they had loaded provisions and their belongings they shot out of Big Spring at a quick trot. Angus cracked the whip over the horses' heads as his blue eyes twinkled over red cheeks. His white beard flapped in the wind as he hooted and hollered.

The unlikely party rode into Abilene less than three

days later and headed for the stables where they could store the buggy.

"Howdy, Angus," Fred Block said. "I see you brought Waldo's buggy. She's a pretty one, ain't she?"

"She's danged fast, too," Angus said as he pushed his foot on the brake lever, set it, and jumped down.

"I ain't seen ya around for a spell, Sheriff," Fred said.

"Oh. I ain't the sheriff of Big Spring no more." Angus chuckled. "I was hoping I could find something here in town."

"Where y'all goin'? To a Wild West show or a circus?" the liveryman asked as the odd characters stretched their legs.

"No, Fred, these be my friends. This here is Jack and his son Del, and this is his best buddy, Tommy," McGee said.

When he turned to introduce Tuc and Potak they had vanished.

"I wonder where that pair got off to?" Angus asked as he pulled on his white beard and looked all around. "They be a funny pair. They always have been and always will be, too. Now that I think about it, I ain't ever seen 'em in a big city."

McGee waved to his traveling partners and said, "Let's warm up a bit. Then, we will head out. Fred's got a pot-bellied stove in the back room. Follow me."

The four sipped coffee and warmed themselves for about an hour. Then, with Fred's directions, they headed out to the Buckhorn Gentlemen's Club.

As they walked toward the exit, Fred called out, "I don't know if they will be open tonight. It's Christmas Eve, Angus. I'm closing up and heading back to the little woman, myself. I hope you find what you are looking for, boys. Blessed tidings to you all."

Another belly laugh trumpeted from the stout and former sheriff. Again, his big belly jiggled. With a twinkle in his eye, he said, "Dadgumit, boys, I plumb lost track of the days. I didn't realize it was Christmas Eve."

"It's always been just another day, as far as I was concerned," Jack said. "But I think this one is going to be special."

He put his arms around the two teenagers as they trudged out into the cold again. "It's the best Christmas I've had ever," Del declared. "And it's going to be the same for you, too, Tommy. Don't worry, we're going to find M."

Young Turnbolt pulled his collar up to block the piercing wind and said, "I sure hope so. What if she doesn't want to see me, though, Del?"

"Don't be stupid, Tommy," his friend said. "She was a bit of a hard case, as I recall, but she loved you. I saw it every day."

"Why do you think she didn't come looking for me?" Tommy asked, his voice hushed and deep.

"When you're an adult, life gets complicated," Jack said as he got a tighter grip on the two boys.

McGee had been listening and stopped abruptly in the middle of the vacant street, put his hands on his hips, and imparted advice only a man of his age could share.

"Listen here, all of ya," he said. "Life is a one-way path. No matter how many detours you take, none of them leads backward. Once you know and accept that, existence is a heap easier. All any of us can do is the best we can with what you have and what you are and what you've become.

"I'm proud of y'all. You've overcome some mighty big odds, especially you boys. Look how far you have come. Have faith. This last stop is going to be as bountiful as the one in Big Spring. After all, it's Christmas!"

Then the big lawman laughed again. His belly bobbed up and down and his beard was tossed in the wind. Jack, Del, and Tommy couldn't help themselves. They laughed with him.

* * *

ALL THE LIGHTS were out at the Buckhorn Gentlemen's Club, but they could hear voices in the back of the large house that had pine garlands along the top of its massive porch.

Jack knocked twice at the big purple door, but nobody answered. He looked forlorn at the others and said, "I guess the liveryman was right. The place is closed up for the holiday. We'll have to come back in a few days."

Tommy was heartbroken and Del felt his pain as the seven-foot teen kicked at a pile of snow and muttered, "I knew it was too good to be true."

"Hold on there just a minute, boys. You can't give up that easily," Angus said. "I can hear voices and singing inside. They must be at the back of the house. Let's see if there's a back door. This time, I'll do the knockin', Jack."

They had to kick through several high snowdrifts to get to the back of the stately house. McGee spotted a yellow glow coming from the back door and motioned for the trio to follow. His feet pounded up a set of wooden steps that led to a back porch and door. Before he knocked, he inhaled deeply, turned to the boys, and said, "Do you smell that, men? I think they're having themselves a Christmas Eve meal in there. Are ya hungry?"

"I am," Jack said.

"Me too," said Delbert.

A disgruntled Tommy said, "Maybe we should just go. They probably don't want to be disturbed."

McGee turned, jammed a fat finger into the chest of the tall teen, and said, "I'd like you to know Sheriff Angus McGee can disturb anyone he darn well pleases, especially when he smells a turkey roasting on a cold Texas night."

"But you ain't a sheriff anymore, Angus," Jack said.

"They don't know that, do they?" he replied, pulled a pistol from his holster, and pounded on the door with the barrel. When nobody responded, he turned the pistol around and banged louder with the butt.

Finally, he heard footsteps and a gray-haired woman opened the door three inches so she could look outside and briskly declare, "The Gentlemen's Club is closed. Come back in two days."

Before she could slam the door shut, Angus shoved his foot in the opening and said, "Just a dag-blamed minute, ma'am. I am Sheriff Angus McGee. I am here on a matter of urgency."

"Why didn't you say that in the first place?" she asked and opened the door wide.

"Why didn't you answer the door when I first knocked?" McGee asked.

"As I said, it's Christmas Eve and we're closed," Miss Lilly replied.

"Well, I'm here to search the premises," Angus said and stepped inside.

"You are a persistent old goat, aren't you?" she said, but couldn't help but smile when she saw the sheriff's rosy cheeks and white beard. "Why didn't you wait until everyone was in bed and slip down the chimney?"

"What are you talking about?" Angus asked, but not without noticing how attractively dressed the woman was. At least a dozen women stood behind her after hearing the commotion the sheriff had created.

Del snickered and said, "She made a joke, Sheriff. Santa Claus usually comes down a chimney on Christmas Eve."

"What? Who? Me? Why I never," the jovial fat man said and burst into laughter so violently his belly bounced up and down like a big ball.

His mirth irritated the matronly owner of the Gentlemen's Club to no end. "If you are done having your laugh at my expense, state your business so we can get back to our party. As the young man said, it is Christmas Eve."

"Go bother someone else," one of the women yelled out.

"You just can't barge in here for no reason," another voice challenged. "Miss Lilly ain't done nothin' wrong."

"Let's not get our bloomers ruffled, here," McGee declared. "We're here to talk to your bearded bartender. What's her name, boys?"

Simultaneously, the boys said her name, "Emily Turnbolt."

A statuesque woman with blonde hair and a magnificent beard, exquisitely coifed, stepped forward and said, "I'm Emily Turnbolt. What do you want with me?"

The boys responded immediately, calling her by the one name she had asked to be called so many years ago. "M!" they shouted with happiness.

She stopped and gaped at the boys, one tall and one small. Then she glanced at the two men and finally at Miss Lilly. Everyone stared in silence.

At last, Jack said, "Emily, I'm Jack Elliott. Years ago, you and my wife, Estar, were good friends working a job you both loved."

Both of Emily's hands covered her mouth to muffle her startled response to such a shocking development.

"I remember you," she said. "Estar was a sweetheart."

"This is our son, Delbert," Jack advised, placing his hand on the small boy's shoulder.

"He looks just like his mother," she said with a smile.

"More importantly, guess who this is," Del said and pointed up to his tall friend.

Emily took a step forward and again covered her mouth as she examined the tall teen from his toes to his face.

"Tommy, is that you?" she said.

When he nodded, she lunged at him, wrapped her arms around his waist, and buried her face in his chest. She wept tears of joy and asked, "How did you find me?"

"It wasn't easy, but Del and me had a lot of help," he said. "Are you really glad to see me?"

"Of course, I've been searching for you ever since I got to Abilene. I'll bet I've sent one hundred telegrams to every city in the Midwest. I've been searching for that despicable Ichabod Justice, hoping he would be able to tell me what happened to you. But I can't find him anywhere."

"That's because he decided to relocate the touring company to California," Del stated. "We left the train somewhere along the Santa Fe Trail and came looking for our parents, that is my dad and you."

"Oh, my goodness," Tommy's mother said. "You came all that way? You're just boys. I don't know how you managed that, but I'm glad you did. This is going to be the best Christmas ever."

Then she turned to Miss Lilly and asked, "Can they stay and have dinner with us? We can't possibly turn them away in this kind of weather."

"I guess, as long as the jolly one over there removes his guns and does me one favor," Miss Lilly said.

Angus looked at the gorgeous woman sideways and asked, "What might that be, ma'am?"

"I want to hear you laugh again, but I want to hear a 'Ho-Ho-Ho!' at the end," she explained.

"What in tarnation for?" he said, a bit put out. The sheriff had never had such a crazy request.

Del grabbed him by the sleeve and motioned for him to lower his ear. When he did, he whispered, "It's to put everyone back in the Christmas spirit, Santa!"

It took the fat man a couple of seconds to get it. Then, he guffawed like he actually was St. Nick. Everybody joined in because his merriment was so infectious.

Then, the discarded sheriff, who reminded everyone

of Santa, joined the prodigal parents, the misfits who were best friends, and the proud women of the Buckhorn Gentlemen's Club for a Christmas celebration that would not soon be forgotten.

17. TONKAWA SOLSTICE

Abilene, Texas

POTAK SMILED AS HE TOOK A BIG BITE OF A DRUMSTICK, and Tuc chewed on a turkey wing. Bones crackled in the warrior's mouth as he devoured the pieces whole. A wicker basket sat between them in a room inside the Abilene livery. The owner was another friend of Angus McGee who had allowed them to spend the night before they departed for southern Texas. A massive stone chimney stood in the corner and warmed the room. The medicine man wrapped himself in a bearskin. The warrior sat bare-chested before the heat. Sweat shone off Tuc's skin as muscles glistened in the dim light.

"I can't wait to get back to warm weather," Potak said. "I don't like walking in the snow."

Both Indians sat on blankets they placed on the sawdust floor beside the roaring fire. The coals inside glowed so brightly that they cast an orange glow on everything in the room. Heat radiated out, making it as warm as freshly baked bread. An abundance of smells came from the basket of food and the aroma filled the air mixed with charred wood.

"Lula makes the best grub I've ever eaten," Potak said between mouthfuls. "Turkey, mushy potatoes with gravy, cranberries, corn on the cob, and she even gave us a pie. She said she made it with pumpkins. Now, I see why the White people like Christmas so much."

"Usually, gringo food is not as good as ours. Lula cooks much better than you, cousin. You should stay a while and let her teach you. We'll eat better then." The criticism made the warrior smile.

"A Christmas meal is not just for White people. It comes from the tribe they called Christians. Their tribe is said to be as vast as the old Cherokee Nation. Some say much larger. Even an Indian can be a Christian. Don't you remember the Mexican padres telling the little children about Christ?"

"I like this celebration, and I am Tonkawa. I don't think you have to be a Christian to like it. With food like this, I believe everybody would like Christmas," Tuc said. Again, a smile touched the edges of his mouth.

No matter what his cousin had to say, Tuc felt compelled to contest or criticize. But Potak knew this was his way, and it didn't mean he didn't care. He had followed him this time to the coldest depths in Texas and without reward. It was a grueling winter, but he went just the same.

When the Tonkawa scouted for the Army or the Texas Rangers, they get paid. They even charged for gossip. During the time of the winter solstice, sharing and helping others in need was customary. Potak felt good about what they had done. For him, the feeling he had inside would suffice for his gratification.

"I wonder why White men don't like us, but some Black people do?" Tuc asked.

Usually, Tuc only complained or talked of battles. Something had brought the philosophical side out in him. It surprised the old medicine man. Tuc focuses on little other than his enemies and those of the old shaman. It was rare he asked a metaphysical question of any depth. At least not such a profound one.

"Most men don't like you because you frighten them, no matter what color they are. You're just like a mean old Indian camp dog." Potak chuckled. "You smell their fear, and your instinct is to frighten them more. You know we have White friends, Black friends, and Red friends, too. I believe White men hated us only because they wanted our land. They wanted our buffalo, our elk, and our deer. If we had nothing they wanted, they would have probably left us to live in peace and we would all be friends.

"The worst tragedy was when they found our gold. Then, they even took places no White man would want to live. It's the way of life, though. Before the Tonkawa, there were other tribes, but we conquered them. Before them, there were others, and those were conquered, too. This is sadly the way of humans everywhere and from the beginning of time. They say the Cherokee Nation is three thousand years old. As you have discovered over the years, we have met many people who are not Indians, and they are also good. Just as we killed evil Indians when it was called on us to do so."

"We did good things this solstice," Tuc said and continued to surprise his cousin. "We helped those boys find their parents. I wonder why the ways of the White world are so strange and complicated?"

* * *

THE FLAMES CARESSED the logs like long fingers as they snapped and crackled. Cinders swirled around and around, disappearing into the twilight. Half a moon showed overhead. It cast long shadows on the hot Texas night. The cousins had returned to the south and warmer weather. They sat on a hilltop from which they could see for miles. Insects and animals of the night rummaged in the bushes. An owl hooted, and another replied.

Tuc tilted his head to one side as he focused on the night creatures. He separated each sound to detect if there was danger. His hooded eyes scoured the night as if his sight could penetrate the dark.

Potak reached into the leather pouch where he kept his corncob pipe, given to him by his mentor decades before. It had survived all the years, just like the two old scouts. He pulled out his tin of herbal mix and filled his pipe. The fire's light reflected off the blade as he selected the perfect size cinder to place in the center of the bowl. In seconds, clouds of smoke swirled around his head as he puffed and puffed.

"What happened to the glass crystal?" Tuc asked after a spell of silence. "I still believe witches gave it to the White boys. I never saw it again after the storm."

"What do you care what happened to the crystal

ball?" Potak asked as he closed his eyes and peered into another world, that of the Indian spirits. "It had a purpose, and that purpose was served. It is as simple as that."

"As long as it's not near me, I don't care where it is," Tuc growled. "I stay clear of witches and demons. They can cast evil spells and make men weak."

"You worry about that which you do not understand. It is said the unknown is what is feared most," Potak replied. "Did you feel weak after our solstice? Didn't we do as the boys asked?"

"You said that's what the Tonkawa spirits would want," Tuc replied. "Now they should be happy and give us a good year."

"Doing good is pointless if you expect a reward in return," the weathered shaman said, opening his eyes. Smoke swirled in his pupils. "Any fool knows that."

"You still haven't answered my question," Tuc said as he tilted his head back and his eyes heavenward.

A series of falling stars streaked across the night and disappeared behind the mountains on the horizon. Trails of heat followed the small meteorites, generating light as they cut bright paths across the sky. The miracles of Mother Nature never ceased to amaze the Tonkawa. They lived their lives as one with the earth and all its wonders.

"And which question was that?" Potak asked as he stared at something much farther away, a place only he could see.

Tuc grumbled at his cousin. "He knew better than to ask more. If he didn't want to answer, he knew he wouldn't. Especially if he really didn't know."

Leaves ruffled overhead, and the old shaman smiled.

They had both fallen into a deep trance-like sleep. The Wandering Tree had returned as Potak had expected. He clutched the leather pouch to his chest. Every few seconds, the tiny orb inside pulsated like a lightning bug, its warmth known only by the old medicine man.

A LOOK AT:

ABANDONED (BENJIE WILLOW
THE ORPHAN1)

A massacre stole everything—the trail to El Paso might give
him a reason to keep going...

Fourteen-year-old Benjie Willow should've died with the rest
of his family. Hidden in a water well as Comanche raiders
swept through his ranch on the Red River, he emerged into a
world he no longer recognized—alone, grieving, and hunted.

When seasoned frontiersman Malvo Tanner and the quiet
Choctaw warrior Chito-Oche spot smoke on the horizon, they
don't expect to find a terrified boy as the only survivor. Taking
Benjie in, they set off for El Paso, dragging him through
lawless lands where danger rides faster than justice...and the
past haunts every mile.

But the West isn't kind to orphans, and as Benjie struggles to
find his place in this brutal new world, he'll have to learn what
it means to survive...not just in body, but in spirit.

Will the trail harden him into something unrecognizable...or
forge a future he never dared to imagine?

AVAILABLE NOW

ABOUT THE AUTHORS

Ash Lingam was born and raised in Southern Ohio, not far from the mighty Ohio River. His family was among the early settlers in pre-Revolutionary America. He has traced his lineage back to around 1746 when his ancestors immigrated from Europe to the aspiring American Colonies.

A retired marketing executive, Ash devotes his spare time to training police dogs and writing novels.

https://www.ashlingam.com/

Gerald L Guy is a retired newspaper editor who lives in Palm Coast, FL, with his wife, Joanne. His pursuit of words began as a sportswriter in his hometown of Warren, Ohio. Guy eventually edited daily newspapers in Ohio, Georgia, and Wisconsin. When he's not writing or editing short stories and novels, he's walking the scenic trails and sunny beaches of Flagler County.

www.storiesbyguy.com